AMONG THE
Volcanoes

AMONG THE
Volcanoes

Omar S. Castañeda

Lodestar Books

DUTTON   NEW YORK

This work was made possible in part by a Central American research grant from the Fulbright Commission.

Library of Congress Cataloging-in-Publication Data

Castañeda, Omar S., 1954–
    Among the volcanoes / Omar S. Castañeda.
        p.   cm.
    Summary: When her mother becomes ill, Isabel, a Mayan girl living in contemporary Guatemala, must care for her and continue her search for her own identity in a world fraught with upheaval and change.
    ISBN 0-525-67332-6
    1. Guatemala—Fiction.   2. Mayas—Fiction.   3. Indians of Central America—Guatemala—Fiction.   I. Title.
PZ7.C26859Am   1991
[Fic]—dc20   90-43874
                                                                        CIP
                                                                        AC

Published in the United States by Lodestar Books,
an affiliate of Dutton Children's Books,
a division of Penguin Books USA Inc.

Published simultaneously in Canada by
McClelland & Stewart, Toronto

Editor: Rosemary Brosnan   Designer: Marilyn Granald, LMD
Printed in the U.S.A.   First Edition
10   9   8   7   6   5   4   3   2   1

This book is dedicated first to my family:
Jill Jepson, Omar Clark, and Bleu Chere;
to my aunt, Eugenia Duarte Méndez, for her kindness;
also to Melissa Rickey, for her advice along the way;
and, very importantly, to
Rosemary Brosnan, for her faith and for her superb
editorial guidance. What errors remain are mine alone.

Author's Note

Three languages other than English are found in this story: Spanish, Tzutujil, and Quiché. The last two are from the language family called Mayan. In Guatemala alone there are some twenty-seven indigenous languages. In Central Guatemala (where the story takes place) the three major languages of Quiché, Cakchiquel, and Tzutujil are not completely incomprehensible between speakers. Tzutujil and Cakchiquel are easily mutually understood; Quiché is difficult for speakers of the other two to understand.

Pronunciation in Mayan generally follows Spanish pronunciation. The following is a brief explanation of some of the more difficult aspects:

> An apostrophe indicates a glottal stop, that is, the blocking of the glottis as in the *tl* in *subtle* or in *bottle*.
> x is like *sh* in English;
> *j* is like *h* in the English *hang;*
> *uu* is like the English *woo;*
> *tz* is like *ts* in the English *bats*

The accent always falls on the last syllable in Mayan. Roughly speaking, then, Tzutujil is Tsoo-too-HEAL.

Originally, Mayan was written in hieroglyphs and not in Latin-based script until near the mid-1500s. Since that time, different orthographic systems have been used in an attempt to systematize difficult sounds (to non-Mayan speakers, that is). Naturally, different signing systems lead to single words being spelled differently. There are also representational systems to enhance literacy, pride, and consistency for the Maya themselves, but much effort, of course, is finally based on value as measured by conformity to European–American conventions and needs.

One

sabel Pacay felt she was walking through a dream. She went gingerly down the dirt avenue from her family's hut and toward the lake's edge. Now and then she heard her father kick a stone, which would clatter down the rocky embankment to the water.

An early morning fog hung like heavy wadding over the entire village, masking her father's steps, masking the path and the thick vegetation looming all around, so that everything in the tiny village seemed more a part of the gossamer landscape of dreams rather than part of the hard shapes and lines of reality.

Isabel remembered sitting, just a few days earlier, with her father on Oro Hill. They had watched with special reverence as the sun burned away the clouds that had loomed over the surrounding volcanoes, until the village of Chuuí Chopaló seemed to bubble up from that white sea one hut at a time. With the slowness of dawn, the small homes of the few hundred families were completely revealed, as were the central clearing between the cut-rock school building, the church with the stone-gray cross in front, and the *cooperativo,* where tools and feed were brought from the distant towns of Santiago Atitlán and San Lucas Tolimán. The clearing was used for recess, town meetings, and anything else that brought everyone out from the small clutch of adobe and thatch huts. On that morning, when she sat on the hilltop with her father, the hard-packed clearing appeared through the draping fog like a bronze platter used by the ancients to make sacred offerings.

"Long ago," her father had intoned solemnly, "our people lived here at the top of the hill in a beautiful city with polished gold jaguars guarding each gate. Their teeth were bright with silver and their eyes were solid jade."

Isabel could only stare up at her father, Alfredo Pacay, as he spoke.

"Everyone knew us then as the people of the Bird House. We came from across the great lagoon and settled here above the water to build our city. That was before the Spanish came." Alfredo uttered a sigh that seemed to roll forever from between his lips.

Isabel loved listening to her father tell of days long past and of traditions fast disappearing. She also loved to hear her teacher, Maestro Andrés Xiloj, explain things about the present world, about places that seemed impossibly far away and just as miraculous as the Mayan villages all around Lake Atitlán—foreign places with names like Orlando, New York, or the tongue-twisting Indianapolis.

Isabel could not afford the luxury of lazy reminiscing. She did not want to lose her father or have him discover that she had left the house so soon after him—like a spy. Yet the beautiful and mysterious fog triggered more memories than she could resist.

She also recalled her father telling how the demigod Maximón sat atop the tallest palace roof as he kept a lookout for the Spanish soldiers and tried to fix his broken marimba. The sticks of the musical instrument acted as if they had a life of their own and scattered from his hands to fall on the slope of the hill. Her father explained that the fallen sticks became the first homes after the conquistadores brought down the walls of the city.

"There's nothing left," her father had whispered. "Like the poc-duck—forever gone."

Isabel thought then that he was about to cry. It was true. If one looked very, very hard, one could still find small glyphs on broken stones, but they were so small and rare that no one looked for them anymore. The ancient walls had fallen long ago; the palace blocks had been broken up to make newer buildings. The wind and rain had eroded virtually all signs of the old splendor, and all that remained up on the hill was the corn and coffee plants of Salvador Tzui's family. Perhaps Salvador had his own sense of loss, since he allowed one stalk of corn, a traditional symbol of their Mayan roots, to remain after each harvest. As for the poc, that bird that neither flew nor walked on land, a symbol of the Maya before any Spanish invasion, it had disappeared without a single trace.

3

All these thoughts came crashing into Isabel's mind because two strange things had occurred that morning: Her mother had stayed on her sleeping mat after Isabel had awakened, and her father had slipped out of the house without his coffee and before Isabel had gone to fetch water. Ordinarily, Isabel awoke soon after her mother. Manuela set to making tortillas while Isabel fetched water. Once the water was carried back and the coffee brought to a boil, Alfredo and the younger children were awakened. Isabel's two brothers and sister would eat a breakfast of scrambled eggs or black beans, coffee, and tortillas.

This time, however, her mother, Manuela, still lay asleep. Her father had already dressed in his maroon and white short pants, iridescent waist sash, and white shirt. He had been pulling on his sandals when Isabel came out from behind the blanket that screened parents from children in their small home.

"*Buenos,*" her father had said—"good," short for "good morning."

He did not wish to wait for his coffee.

"And Mother?" she had asked.

"She's not feeling well. You'll have to take care of things."

"I'll make breakfast for you."

"No. There's no time." His hand reached out to gently squeeze her arm above the elbow. And then he left.

She did not know what was troubling him, exactly, but that he was definitely troubled was clear in the way he bent to his sandal straps, the way his hand electrified her arm, and the way his face turned into a dark flower of shadows. She didn't know it then, but that sorrowful look on his face was the same look she now—following at a spy's distance—remembered he wore while watching the sun burn through the fog the other day. It was a look of sadness over the loss of something irreplaceable.

She had waited for him to get a head start; then she followed at a short distance, well hidden by the fog. The dense white cushioned noises, deadened sounds, and, long after sunset, so blinded normal activities that it was just an added reason not to walk at night. The other reason was that the guerrilla activity up the volcano had brought down a government curfew and occasional gunfire. In some of the other *aldeas,* or hamlets, men had been killed during the night. When it happened, the government soldiers came into each *aldea* and gave a speech about the evil guerrillas and those unfortunate men who collaborated with them. The sergeant or captain would lift his gun into the air and remind everyone of the curfew. One of his men would then post an order from General Ramos for all those who were literate. Isabel read for her family, but the posted bulletin always said exactly what the sergeant had said. Isabel sometimes suspected there was no General Ramos at all and that the sergeant made all of it up to give force to his own ambitions. Isabel reminded herself that the morning, though foggy and quiet, was a time that was safe from political intricacies. She cocked her ears to better track her father.

They descended the avenue that wound its way to the small inlet where the men kept their wooden skiffs for fishing and for hugging the shoreline between villages. She heard the dull crunch of gravel beneath her father's sandaled feet. She walked barefoot, as she always did, a tall urn balanced on a patch of cloth on her head. Her long black hair swished like a horse's tail to her lower back. She wore a *huipil,* a white blouse with red, blue, and green brocade at the collar. On one shoulder she wore a folded shawl that hung below her waist in front and back. Her wrap-around skirt went to her ankles. It was dark blue-green, with silver wound throughout. The poor hem had frayed months ago, but the family did not have either the money to buy clothing or the time to make her new clothes, for Isabel spent more and more time doing her mother's chores and taking care of her mother's requests. Isabel always repaired her siblings' clothing before her own. By being the first, she was now last. And last not only in receiving material things, but in receiving what she most dearly wanted and could least explain.

Already too many days had passed since she had gone to school. She missed hearing her friend Teresa cry out: "Isabel, are you going today? How's your mother feeling? How are your father and brothers and sister? Hurry; we'll walk together."

"Not today, Teresa."

Teresa would come early to tell Isabel all the strange things Maestro Xiloj had taught them in her absence. Isabel would listen so intently that she would nearly forget the silver stars Teresa had recently had implanted in her front teeth, stars that sparkled in her mouth when she spoke or laughed.

"I can't go," Isabel would have to say.

6

Isabel tried concentrating on following her father, but something inside her knew all these entwining thoughts were braided, somehow, with her father's sudden departure. How, she could not guess. Her mother's illness had worsened over the past few days, until Isabel now spent more time nursing at home than with her friends or at school learning about the whole bewildering world from Andrés Xiloj. She knew it was wrong to complain, and she never did—at least not out loud. And when she resented the loss of time from school and from her friends, she felt ashamed, as if she were doing something terrible to her mother and to the rest of her family. She was the oldest child. She had duties. She was already at an age when marriage was expected, not idle desires to become a teacher. Sometimes, however, the duties were too much for her. She didn't feel smart enough or old enough to handle everything. Not yet, anyway. She wanted to be smart, to learn more first. She wanted to fill up this thing inside her that always dreamed and always made associations like now, between these memories and thoughts and the curious actions of her father.

High above Isabel, out of sight because of the fog, a flock of parrots squawked. She imagined their bright green feathers catching the gray light that smears up the sky, which is the First Dawn, the first brightening. Sometimes Isabel wished she could be a bird with the power to fly up and away from the problems not only of her village, but those problems within her own family. She imagined as a bird she might never have to be solely responsible for anything except herself. As a quetzal, the spirit of the Maya against all foreign invaders, she would be elegant and nobler than the life she was born into, and she would wing over the vast wall of volcanoes surrounding the lake and discover the world spreading infinitely outward.

Isabel suddenly stopped when she did not hear her father's step. They stood a dozen meters apart, though completely hidden from each other. Isabel had the advantage. She often walked out in the morning for water. Her father did not usually go out until the invading white bank had drifted across the lake and up the slopes of Sololá. Now neither of them moved. The only sounds were of the receding parrots and the soft clicking of insects. Finally, Alfredo Pacay continued on; Isabel followed more carefully, more observantly.

She tracked the footfalls to the sound of water lapping the shore and crouched near the boats. Her father's figure appeared suddenly from the white curtain. He struggled with his bag there by the water and fished out one of their hens. Isabel was more startled by the fact that she hadn't heard him get one of the chickens, or heard the animal fluttering inside the bag, than by the simple fact that he had brought one to the launching site of his dugout canoe. The chicken's claws were tied with a blue string.

Isabel craned her neck to watch her father begin a prayer that instantly frightened her:

Oh Lord, help me and my family.
Lord God, Heart of Sky, Heart of Earth,
give my daughter strength, give her courage
to not err, to not make a false step.
Accept from me this sacrifice

and this plea for you to show her
the clear way, the white way.

Isabel saw him cut into the bird's collar and the blood
leap out like a red ribbon from its throat. Her father
had his eyes pressed tightly shut. His lips moved in
prayer as he held the hen downward so the blood poured
into a clay dish by his feet. He prayed for some time,
too quietly for her to hear his words; then he ended
loudly with:

> Lord God, Heart of Heaven, Father.
> Your will here as in Heaven.
> Amen.

Isabel clutched the trunk of the tree for support. Her
legs felt weak and rubbery. The sight of her father making the sacrifice to the old gods as well as to the Christian god brought chills up and down her arms. She had
heard similar prayers before. Even during mass, when
Father Ordoño came from Santiago, the prayers were
mixtures of the old and new. What frightened Isabel
was not the blend, but that the prayer was said for her.
The animal had died on her behalf. Her father held
some dread for her! This is what rocked her back.

It could only mean that her mother was worse than
she had thought. It meant that the *sanjorín,* the village
healer, had not been as successful as they had all expected. And it meant that Isabel would be more bound
to the nursing of her mother and the care of her father
and siblings than before.

Alfredo let the blood run into the dish. He sprinkled

flower petals on the blood and lit a misshapen chunk of dark incense. Once the dark smoke licked its steady way into the sky, he knelt with hands clasped in prayer. Again the words were muffled by the distance and by his huddling body. He made of his closed shape a private alcove for prayer.

Even so, Isabel heard him repeat over and over the name *Chopaló,* the word actually two words: *cho,* meaning "lake," and *paló,* meaning "sea" in old Quiché. But the prayer made the words into one, so that it was an ardent voicing, a plea to the forces and spirits of all waters, all lakes and seas. It didn't matter whether they were saltwater or fresh, bay, lagoon, or estuary. For the villagers, as for so many of the peoples of Guatemala, water was so basic and important a need that it was a force—a god!—everyone urgently prayed to. When said as *Lake-sea,* one word, it became the name of a divine force, one that controlled the life and death of every village and town, every group of people that depended on farming. It was a force that governed the richness of the soil and the fullness of crops that grew from the earth. It was a spiritual entity that blessed or that terrorized with its absence. It was this eternal spirit that lent its name to Isabel's village: Chuuí Chopaló, Above the Lake-sea—the village resting on the slopes of volcanoes above beautiful Lake Atitlán.

In these words, unlike Alfredo's first prayer, Isabel sensed promise and hope. She had always loved to hear the words, to feel the sound like birdsong on her own tongue—Ch-woo-EE Cho-pah-LO: above the Lake-sea, above the life-giving waters. The curious chirping of the name echoed the call of some unknown bird—

the bird she might become: the quetzal of the warrior Tecún Umán, who had fought against Pedro Alvarado, the Spanish conqueror with strange horses, and had lost. The chirping of the name Chuuí Chopaló gave her the sensation of a bird that flew high above the waters, soaring free above any danger, any misfortune. The name bestowed this hope to the village itself.

Her father placed the dish and bird into his boat and slid the craft past the mudbank. Isabel whispered the name to herself—Chuuí Chopaló. She watched her father push against the wood gunwales, and the boat scraped one final time before gliding effortlessly onto water. Alfredo took several steps in the water and then lifted himself into the boat. "Chuuí Chopaló," Isabel said again to herself. Her father's shoulders leaned into some search within the boat; then he lifted an oar to dip alongside the launch. Within a few strokes, her father stood up and continued oaring in this more usual way. He slipped easily out of sight.

Everything was quiet. The oar dipped silently into water. The boat sent back to shore a gentle and silent wake over the underwater stones. The sun ascended quietly, and the dawn sprayed a handful of light, some of which skimmed the surface, some of which sank to bounce off the blue and green stones. The flood of fog, earlier inundating every nook and cranny of the village, began evaporating as Isabel stood rock still by the water. Slowly, Isabel began to wish the light of dawn would enter her body and germinate there a pair of gorgeous quetzal wings, which would grow out from her shoulders. Oh, she would lift away from shore then. She would really fly then.

"Chuuí Chopaló," she whispered.

Two

Isabel waited until her father was well out of earshot before bending to push the lip of her urn underwater. It took that amount of time to get herself under control, to get her mind away from the simple desire to fly away from troubles, and to realize she must face her duties. She must help her mother, no matter how much it cost her. And so, with resolve, she forced away the volcanic white rocks floating by the shore, which threatened to cork up the urn's throat. The water rushed down the narrow neck in huge gulps, to finally gurgle and spit when the urn was full. It took nearly all her strength to lift it up to her head for carrying, but once it rested atop the patch of cloth, she felt perfectly at ease with it. She stepped up the bank and onto the rocky path, one hand placed gently against the side of the clay urn.

From behind, she might have looked like a dancer or

gymnast proving her great acrobatic skill, but she was no different from any of the other girls or women in her village. A full-grown woman could carry more than fifty pounds on her head—uphill, barefoot, and for a few miles. A young woman like Isabel was nearly as capable. Even her baby sister, Marcelina, occasionally would help by carrying straw baskets full of tortillas, food for her brothers in the fields, or clothing to sell to the artisan merchants in Santiago Atitlán. From the age of two, girls would playfully lift stones to their heads or stack finished plates of beans on their skulls, steady them with one hand, and walk to the water urns where older sisters helped mothers clean up after meals. While playing, little girls would wear their shoulder scarves on their heads in case some errand was given to them.

Already other girls and mothers were coming down the pathways to reach the lake. Isabel loved this time of morning. The air seemed to sparkle not only because of the new sun brightening across the water, the red and white flowers speckling through trees, or the glinting of light from iridescent stones, but because the very air came alive with the activity of waking people. She could almost hear the village stretch itself awake as the sun peeked over the mountains and groan to get its blood circulating, as if it were some large, slumbering person. She sometimes imagined the village as the prankster Maximón, shifting one leg, stretching his arms way up over his head, and arching his back to finally shake loose sleep's hold on him. All around, doors opened, voices called softly to children or husbands, and the rich odor of wood fires curled its way over the branch fencings, between huts, and down the narrow avenues like some thread luring Isabel to her own home fire through that tight maze of neighbors.

It was for these reasons that Isabel often awoke earlier than anyone else in the village. Mornings were peaceful, beautiful, almost magical. They promised something bright.

"Isabel," she heard. *"Buenos!"*

"Buenos, Eugenia."

The two friends waved to each other across the expanse of the dirt avenue, one homeward bound and the other lakeward bound. Eugenia and Isabel had been schoolmates until Eugenia got married and went to live with her new husband's family. It was so common for girls in their middle and late teens to get married that very few girls ever continued school. Usually it was the wealthiest families or the ladino families—mixed Mayan and Hispanic—that allowed their children to continue and become teachers. In families like Isabel's, the idea was ridiculous. These families needed the children for hard work in the coffee fields and the cornfields.

"You go by so fast without a word about your mother?" another voice reprimanded.

Isabel turned to see Doña Consuela leaning over the short fence surrounding her stuccoed hut. Her face was deep brown and etched with intricate wrinkles. Her eyes were like the black *zompopo* ants.

"Utz awach?" Isabel asked in Tzutujil how the old woman was; at the same time, she respectfully cast her glance downward.

"Utz, thank you," she answered curtly, still expecting news of Isabel's mother.

"She is strong." Isabel would not look up.

"Better?"

"Thanks be to God, she is strong."

Doña Consuela coughed heavily and spat.

Isabel dutifully would not move until the older woman dismissed her.

"Tell her that to cure the evil eye she must pass a fresh egg over her body and say three Our Fathers. Break the egg in a pan and place it under her bed when she sleeps. In the morning, bury the egg far away from the house."

"Yes, señora."

"And give my best to your family."

"Yes, señora."

"And to you."

But these last words were said with such a distracted voice that Isabel knew she would speak again. Isabel whispered her thanks.

"Time to leave school," the old woman stated flatly, as if there were no other choice and nothing more to say.

And for once, remembering her father's anxious pleas to Chopaló, Isabel felt that perhaps, finally, regrettably, this was true. She lifted her eyes to look into the old woman's face. Maybe she would see in those ancient lines a map to help her find a way out.

"Go on now," Doña Consuela said, shooing her with a wave of her fingers.

"Maltioch"—"thanks."

The sun now had an edge of painful intensity. Everything seemed too bright, too revealing, as Isabel worked her way back home. There was no way to leave the future in shadows. She approached the familiar fence made of cornstalks lashed together with vines and found herself gulping air to still her pounding heart.

The sounds from inside told her that her brothers and sister were already awake. Isabel whiffed the plume of smoke coming from her home. Her mother hadn't started cooking. The children would be anxious, though quiet. They didn't really understand what was happening to them, but they knew enough to not make trouble. Their mother's weariness and strain were always evident. And not one of them, no matter how tired or frustrated, wanted to bring any added darkness to her eyes.

"Oh, Lord," Isabel said under her breath. She lifted the thin cord of the gate; it leaned open on its rickety leather hinge. At the doorway, she was greeted by Marcelina's little squeal. Isabel barely had time to bring the heavy urn down from her head. Marcelina ran into the warmth of Isabel's skirt and hugged her face into the cloth. Their mother looked up from working a thin branch into the fire.

"I'll do it," Isabel said, moving forward with Marcelina still clinging affectionately.

Her mother leaned on one knee as she lumbered up. "It's going."

"Well, rest. Please, Mamita."

"Impossible." She urged Marcelina away. "Let your sister go. She needs to work."

Near the cleared area where they usually ate together, her mother leaned forward and breathed heavily. Her arms squeezed tightly against her chest as if she were trying desperately to give herself a bear hug.

16

José and Diego stared up from the ground, not daring to say a word to their mother.

Isabel took a step forward, then stopped, afraid that her mother would simply shrug off the attention, pretend again as if it were nothing at all, as if she were perfectly all right.

"Mami, please," Isabel urged. "Sit. Rest."

"I'm okay." Yet as she spoke, she shifted down against the wall and onto the hard-packed earth that was their floor. "Don't worry about me. See to your brothers and sister."

Marcelina clung to her mother's skirt. "Mami?" she asked in her small voice.

And then Manuela smiled widely and looked at the younger children. "What?" she demanded in pretended anger. "Are you ready for school? Don't you want to eat? Then why are you just sitting there? Huh?"

The children grinned back.

"Help your sister," she said to Marcelina.

Isabel took Marcelina's outstretched hand and pulled her close to the fire. It was set in a hollow between three stones, with the stones holding up a flat metal disk. This served as the griddle for tortillas, eggs, and anything that could be cooked on a stove, including pots of water to be boiled.

Marcelina stepped up beside her sister and grabbed hunks of *masa*—dough made of black, yellow, or white corn, ground on a flat, volcanic-stone mortar called a *metate*. The dough was mixed with mineral–lime water and then slapped into the familiar round, flat breads. Marcelina still couldn't make as round or as thin a tor-

17

tilla as Isabel could, but she managed to make them well enough and dropped them onto the fiery hot disk, dusted with more mineral–lime. There, the dough sizzled and sent up a delicious aroma that made all of them hungry.

The oldest boy, José, went outside to gather eggs. Diego looked into the sleeping niches of the black-speckled hen that loved to stay inside. She never laid her eggs inside, but Diego looked to show that he, too, could help.

Their mother wiped a ragged cloth across her face.

Everything seemed natural enough; yet Isabel cooked with one eye on her mother. She could tell the pain was getting worse. The memory of her father at the lake acted like a magnifying glass to every small wince her mother made, every private gesture of agony as her mother's body went through its terrible rebellion. Isabel poured a glass of water into a cup and gave it to her.

"Maltioch."

"I'll finish and walk Marcelina to school."

Isabel turned the tortillas, then scrambled the six eggs José had found. She watched her mother's face for signs that would tell her how bad she felt and to see if there was any chance of speaking to her about what she had been harboring for days.

Her mother fussed with the boys' hair and shirts, whisking away imperfections invisible to anyone but a mother.

"I haven't been to school for several days," Isabel tentatively began, hoping that the words sounded neither like a statement nor a question, but had a little bit of both so that her mother would hear it the way she

18

wanted her to hear it. It was a test of mood, an angling with bait. She stirred the simmering black beans.

Manuela didn't say a word.

The eggs let out a hiss as they hit the metal, and a gust of steam wafted up. Isabel quickly used her wooden spatula to pull the eggs closer to the rim and further away from the too-hot center.

"Go to school, go to school," Marcelina sang, oblivious to the quiet testing going on around her.

Isabel turned to hide her irritation.

"She can't go today," her mother said.

Isabel enjoyed her little sister's pouting at the proclamation.

"But why?" Marcelina whined.

"Get the plate."

Marcelina received the tortillas Isabel held out. The eggs were then scraped into another dish and the pot of beans brought to the eager children. Isabel began serving her siblings, but Manuela motioned that she would do it. The children watched with a mixture of pleasure and concern as their mother served each of them a fair helping without so much as a wince or balk. Her usually arthritic wrists held up the heavy pot, and she didn't flinch once.

"Thank you," they each said in turn.

"To God," their mother added as each one spoke.

The sound of children playing on their way to school came over the fence as they ate. Diego wanted to hurry and meet up with friends. José at twelve, was already one of the last of his group to remain in school. Because of that, he would have preferred going out on the threadlike paths winding in all directions from the village, to arrive at the cornfields where his father bent forward, hoe in hand, to do battle with ever-invading weeds. José enjoyed struggling for that magical balance between tiller and tilled. He helped his father, as they all had, to repay the gods of wind, rain, soil, and all the elements that controlled the lives of farmers. It was with profound joy that José put his hands against the earth and let rich soil seep between his fingers. Even helping his father cut firewood to sell, or boating out to fish, was far more attractive than school to him.

Isabel felt as intensely as her brother, but in reverse. It wasn't really school that enthralled her, but learning, listening, seeing how diverse and curious the peoples of the world actually were. To her, going to school was like gazing dreamily into a quiet pond and reflecting on the bewildering universe, or it was like flying high above everything and looking where others could not. This was something she tried explaining to her boyfriend, Lucas Choy, and always she felt as if she had almost explained it, nearly, just about . . . but not quite. Fortunately, he loved her enough to occasionally listen in Maestro Xiloj's classroom. Really, he went to see her, and only when he could leave his work, but she secretly hoped all the wonderful things the teacher talked about would somehow filter into him and mix into his emotions the way they churned and whipped in her like the afternoon waves on Lake Atitlán.

However, in their world, in the village of Chuuí Chopaló, school was a luxury few could afford. The families of the Bird House people had been living and dying in the very same homes for a thousand years, and formal schooling was a relatively recent thing, which usually implied change. In Chuuí Chopaló, change always had something of fear housed within its bright skin.

When Isabel looked at her brother's face, which showed his longing to be in the fields, she understood his desire, though they desired different things. At bottom, the need was the same: to connect with something important in the world; to feel a part of something larger and more necessary than a single person. All this was what being a teacher meant to her.

Diego finished and scuttled outside. José, on the other hand, loped toward the door with a dream of freshly turned earth settling into his mind.

"Take your sister," Manuela commanded.

José turned back. "Me?"

Manuela lifted herself and gathered a few plates. "Take your sister."

Marcelina forked a final mouthful of egg and joined José, after kissing Isabel and her mother.

Isabel stood at the door a moment to watch them leave. Diego was already out of sight. Clumps of children, two to four in a group, moved down the path to the main avenue, which ascended straight toward the rise of the village and further to the base of Oro Hill, where the ruins lay. Past that, it was a twenty-minute walk to the dirt road running between the main towns along the perimeter of Lake Atitlán. Isabel turned quickly to look at her mother.

Manuela had already stacked the plates and now scooped crumbs into her hand. She moved to the home altar.

Isabel turned her attention back outside, where her friend Teresa walked with Ishpuch.

21

"The animals need feeding," her mother said behind her.

"Yes, Mami." Isabel fetched the hemp bag of feed for the chickens. They were fed once each day, like the pig. The animals then spent the rest of the day foraging on their own for what creatures and grains they could find.

Manuela rubbed the crumbs of egg and tortilla and the remaining bean juice around a groove in a heavy gray stone. She fed the stone's mouth so that the deity would continue protecting her against the illness wracking her body. The *sanjorín,* Eziquel Coxol, had given them the stone after burning pine needles and incense and after feeding the mouth with Venado, the local clear liquor. It had taken her father, Alfredo, two hours to move the heavy rock from the healer's hut to their home.

"Never go a day without feeding the stone," Coxol had prescribed.

They had placed flowers and candles around the altar. Alfredo had carefully left a half pint of unopened Venado. He asked the healer if he should also give cigars, but Coxol told him, "It is not Maximón for you to bring cigars and rum. Don't dress it up with scarves and hats, either. Feed it every day; that is all. Pray. And light candles. Do as I say, or I do not know what might happen to your wife."

"Yes," Alfredo said reverently, apologetically.

"That is all?" Manuela had asked, clutching her ribs to hold in her heart, which seemed ready to explode from its cage.

"For now," had been the simple response. "For now."

Isabel had not liked that response then, and she liked it less after watching her father by the lake and while watching her mother struggle across the room to dab food across the thick-lipped stone. Her mother had eaten grilled crickets at each meal for three days to cure attacks, but it did not help. Now they fed the stone's maw. All they could do was wait and pray and hope for change.

"Why did Father leave so early?" she asked her mother's back.

Manuela did not turn. She was frozen in one of her painful clenches: She had described them as her insides tightening, then bubbling, her arms tickling and aching, and her breath like a thing of substance rasping in and out of her lungs.

Isabel stepped quickly to hug her and to soothe the convulsion. It passed quickly, but not without making her mother stagger back to the chair.

"I'm fine," she wheezed.

Isabel got her water.

"I'm fine," she repeated, eyes closed, sweat beading on her forehead.

"I'm going to get the *sanjorín.*"

"I'm fine, really." Her mother's arms suddenly wrapped around her chest and she squeezed through a new spasm, a deeper spasm, a spasm that looked to burst through her skull. "I'm . . . fine," she blurted.

But Isabel was already out the door.

Three

There was such a commotion in the clearing that the entire village seemed to be a tightly coiled rope wrapped around a center full of discord. Isabel had to traverse the clearing to reach the home of Eziquel Coxol. She would have to wade through the snarl of bystanders.

At first she saw nothing, only heard voices in debate. One voice had a very odd accent as he spoke Spanish; the other she recognized as the raspy voice of Don Nicolás Cauec, the appointed mayor of the *aldea*. He spoke Spanish well, better than most in Chuuí Chopaló, and his Tzutujil was excellent.

"Please," the odd voice pleaded. "I mean you no harm."

Isabel spliced into an opening. The foreigner stood beside the church cross with his arms outstretched. He pleaded with Don Nicolás. The young man's hair was blond, wavy, and cut longer than most males in the village would ever wear their hair. His clothes were the kind she had seen in Santiago Atitlán when the boat of tourists arrived from Panajachel. This young man looked like many of those foreigners who stepped off onto the dock and spread out into the shops along the main street. A few would go all the way up the hill to the market and walk around with their packs on their backs, with ripped clothing and cameras. A very small number would be able to say a few words in Tzutujil or Cakchiquel and would ask questions about gods and stories. And they were always excited to pay so much for things Isabel thought ready to be thrown away. She had seen this, but had never dared to speak to a foreigner. It was frowned upon. And now here was this man in her village.

Beside Don Nicolás, the foreigner's face seemed like that of a boy, though he was taller than any man in the village. Even more startling than his pleading manner and presence were his blue eyes, which were like the eyes of blinded animals or cooked fish. The pale color seemed a cloud or mist spreading over his eyes. Isabel first thought he might be blind and carefully watched to see if he moved his head like a blind person— weaving it slightly through the air to focus on sounds and to sense without eyes what was occurring around him. But he moved like anyone else, except that his arms flashed out more, his hands looped over his hips, his legs were spread apart.

Don Nicolás, on the other hand, kept his arms near his body, his legs planted firmly and respectfully close to each other. The older man's hands would never rest on his hips—unless the discussion reached a very disagreeable point. Then it might turn into something terrible, violent. The men of Lake Atitlán were slow to anger, yet when fully angered they were as dangerous as ocelots.

Isabel nearly forgot why she had come this far until she heard the man explain in weary and broken Spanish: "I am medical student, on grant."

She quickly looked at all the faces gathered round to see if Eziquel was also observing this intrusion. It was then that she noticed her best friend, Teresa, standing directly across from her. Isabel waved, but Teresa focused intently on the foreigner. The teachers behind her, including Xiloj, tried to get the students into the classrooms, particularly the youngest ones, but every time one pack of students was herded toward the stone and laminated-metal building, another pack turned back to watch the strange man by the old church cross. She would have no opportunity to speak with Maestro Xiloj or anyone else. Teresa seemed too intent to notice anything around her; her lips were pressed in concentration.

The men beside Isabel spoke among themselves in Tzutujil:

"How can we know who he is?"

"Every sixteen days someone is killed by the army for being a guerrilla."

"It has been sixteen days."

"I don't believe that. It's just stories."

"Then why is this man here in our village?"

And then, as if understanding this peripheral conversation, the American explained again. "I have a grant of Allied Health Organization. I have papers. And letter of introduction." He searched through his pack and handed Don Nicolás a sheet of paper.

"Just in English?"

"I'll read it."

Nicolás Cauec raised his eyebrows in doubt. The American began his translation, but Don Nicolás motioned for him to stop.

"How do we know what this says?"

"Please," the man said again, palms upturned to all of them.

Isabel tried to listen while at the same time scanning the faces for Eziquel. She was glad to see so many of her schoolmates. She wished that her mother would be well so that she could simply enter the room with Maestro Xiloj and sit at the small chair in front of the desk. The small chair had its own board, on which she rested her writing tablet. In one corner, a name had been carved so long ago that it had been all but polished away by sleeves and books: *Charles Walter*, it read. Everyone assumed the desk had come from the United States.

The American began naming people in the hospital in Sololá and doctors in San Lucas Tolimán. Isabel recognized only one name. The names meant little to the men of Chuuí Chopaló. What mattered was exactly what the men beside Isabel pointed out: The activity at night had grown worse; the killings had increased because of the elections not far away; any strange thing could mean new measures taken by the government against the hamlets and towns; what did they have to

27

gain by cooperating; and think of what they might lose. Each of them knew someone who had been killed and left on the road. Some bodies were found without hands or feet. It was a way to disgrace the soul of a person and disgrace his family. Foreigners could only mean trouble. Why was he to be trusted by any of them? Yes, what did they have to gain by allowing him in the village?

"This doesn't prove anything," Don Nicolás said, voicing all of their fears as he waved at the other man's little piece of paper.

"I can help you! I can bring medicine! I can improve your lives!"

The teachers had the students under their wings and were leading the flocks into their classrooms. Several men spoke in Tzutujil about the American's arrogance. One man said such pride could only be the beginning of trouble. Why take chances?

The American pulled out another piece of paper, this one written in Spanish.

" 'To Whom It May Concern,' " Don Nicolás read. " 'Mr. Allan Waters is in Guatemala to conduct a research project for the Allied Health Organization in order to complete a degree in the United States. Your cooperation and assistance will be appreciated, as such projects generally have great benefits for both Guatemala and the individual researcher. If you have any questions or need further information, please contact the United States Information Agency.' " Nicolás looked up. "Where are they?"

The American pointed at the bottom of the page. "In the embassy."

"The United States embassy?"

Allan Waters nodded.

"I'm sorry," Don Nicolás said. "Here in Guatemala, organizations always seem to have at least two faces."

The American glanced desperately at the people around him, who turned slowly away to school, back to work, down paths leading to fields. The crowd gradually shredded itself, to leave the American standing with papers in hand like a windswept scarecrow with tattered sleeves. He half spun on his heels to take in his loneliness, and in that turn his eyes caught Isabel staring. For a moment it seemed he would approach her and begin his pleading all over again. And for a moment, Isabel, too, almost spoke, despite the fear lodged like a stone in her throat. She saw in him a chance to learn about his country, to hear his language come tumbling from his mouth, to see what manner of demon he was.

But she turned from him, sensing someone watching. Teresa was no longer in sight. Isabel's gaze swept the area, the remaining faces, and fell on Lucas Choy, who was watching her every move. He had been standing still, noting the barely perceptible exchange between Isabel and the tall foreigner; then he waited until she noticed him. He did not smile.

"Lucas!" she exclaimed, his name leaping from her like a bird fluttering free of brush. She hurried toward him.

He came forward, too, holding his machete in his left hand.

They stood a respectable distance apart, and only Lucas noticed the lone American drift up the avenue toward the main road. Isabel stood with her palms together.

"How is your mother?"

Isabel shook her head. "I think she's getting worse, Lucas. I don't know what will happen."

He looked past her shoulder. "Give her my regards, please."

"And mine to your family," she said formally.

They had to behave well in public, but this was an uncommon stiffness and formality. They had already said so many things to each other. Why would he act this way? After he and Teresa broke off their engagement, it was assumed that he and Isabel would someday be married. He had proposed. He had already plotted land for their future household. He had already asked her to finish with school and become the woman of the house. It was time, he had said, as others had, too. And more than once, they had held each other in the darkness away from anyone's eyes. His arms were like branches, he was so strong. He always kissed with his eyes open. He stared so deeply into her when he kissed that she felt him loosen the capstone inside her and let free a torrent of crystalline waters.

Isabel blushed with the memory of one particular shadow-veiled meeting.

"You haven't been in school," he said.

"My mother," she said by way of explanation. She wondered why he wouldn't know that. "She hasn't allowed me to go."

Lucas nodded stiffly.

She felt uncomfortable in front of his questioning glare. "I have to find Eziquel Coxol."

"I haven't seen him."

"No, I mean I'm going to his house."

"I see."

She tried again: "Because my mother is worse."

"Then you had better go."

Isabel felt her spine tingling and the blood rushing to her face. She could not believe he would merely turn and walk away. "Lucas," she whispered, bringing up her longing from deep inside her, "I miss you."

But Lucas Choy stepped aside so she could hurry to the *sanjorín's* home.

"What—" she began, then saw in his face a wall that he was not about to tear down. She searched his eyes, but he refused to meet hers. "What's the matter?"

He looked up the path. "You'd better hurry if your mother is ill."

"But what—"

"Is she really ill?" he challenged.

"Of course!"

"Then shouldn't you hurry?"

She felt her mother's illness gobbling time and running in the face of her desire to stand there until he told her what the problem was. His body jagged away from her. His arms folded across his chest; the machete blade dangled by his thigh. Isabel stumbled back from him, walking awkwardly toward the old city ruins and to the mysterious hut where Eziquel Coxol lived.

Behind her, Lucas Choy moved quietly away.

Four

In spite of herself, she felt resentment toward her mother's illness simply because it prevented her from returning to Lucas Choy and not budging until he explained exactly what was going on between them. Her irritation was a hot red pebble that she twirled on her tongue as she hurried up the winding path to the home of the healer, Eziquel Coxol.

His path was narrow, winding like a spurious rivulet between the rock embankments and among the gnarled roots of *hormigo* and *buenaleña* trees. As she ascended, the common birds squabbled among themselves. Blackbirds with long, split tails screamed their two-tone song at the smaller yet more aggressive brown sparrows. Above an adjacent plateau, a turkey buzzard winged through its patient and solitary spiral. Fat lizards with iridescent blue hindquarters scurried in advance of her step. And

among the jacaranda blossoms, a storm of black butter-
flies with transparent wings swirled like the eddies in
the afternoon lake, stirred up by the southern wind—
the *xocomil*. Though these were the most ordinary of
things in Chuuí Chopaló, ascending as she was to the
house of the mystical Eziquel, Isabel felt a ripple traverse her body because of nature's activity. It seemed
impossible for nature to be so casual so near the home
of one of her cohorts. Things could not be what they
appeared in the vicinity of someone who spoke directly
to the gods and who had power over the bric-a-brac of
nature. What seemed normal to Isabel surely was only
hiding its secret face. After all, couldn't this man read
the days and stars and judge the auguries of the calen-
dar brought from the most ancient reaches of the Maya?
Wasn't he mother–father and diviner? She walked
faster, not wanting to spend more time than necessary
on the ambiguous path bridging her world and Coxol's
den of magic.

Seconds before she saw the cornstalk hut squatting
below the pines like just more underbrush, she smelled
the sweet tree-sap incense used in prayers. She approached more tentatively, fearful that she would inter-
rupt some anguished client and yet more than a little
anxious over her own mother's welfare. Muffled voices
carried through the vine-lashed walls and across the
short distance between the simple hut and Isabel, who
stood among the trees. Behind this hut there was another, smaller hut, barely visible to Isabel. It was where
Eziquel lived. The front hut served only for healing and
praying.

She stepped closer to hear and to make out the amorphous shadows moving behind the gaps in the wall. There were two people: one, Coxol; the other, a woman on her knees in front of the long altar. A censer filled with incense smoked heavily beside her. The woman was naming her ancestors, which meant that she had barely begun her prayer. It could be more than an hour before she finished. Coxol sat in the opposite corner of the doorway, at his divining table. His voice commingled with the woman's only as a sort of punctuation to her pleas and her naming of the various forms of God. Isabel still did not recognize the woman, but more importantly, she saw that she might be able to catch Eziquel's attention from the doorway without disturbing her or breaking her devotion.

At the entranceway, Isabel recognized her as a Cakchiquel woman from Santiago Atitlán. She had married a Tzutujil and moved to that town, only to have her husband disappear. She prayed for his safety as Isabel motioned behind her.

Isabel waited at the door until Eziquel deigned to notice her. Standing there, she heard the low grunting or growl of the obsequious hummingbirds. They were difficult to see despite their large size, though their frantic and surprisingly loud wingbeat could be heard everywhere. Finally, Eziquel moved toward her. He spoke first.

"I do not harm. I only cure."

Isabel started at this odd statement. It was unrequested and totally irrelevant to her. She wondered briefly if he knew who she was; then she dismissed the comment for her more urgent errand. "My mother is

34

having another attack," she said. "She is getting worse, Don Eziquel."

He cast a glance at the woman inside. "They are punishing her. She must come and do things in the world."

"My mother?"

Behind the *sanjorín*, the altar sparkled with flickering candlelight. The long wood bank divided the universe into the celestial deities and the terrestrial deities: The top had photos of Coxol's family among large Catholic icons, and candles were lined before the saints and apostles; below, several large stones with mouths and eyes were draped with pine twigs, and before each of these were incense pots and cigars. To one side of the earthly stone images, a wicker basket bulged with empty Venado and Quetzalteca bottles. "Doing things in the world" meant coming here to pray and make offerings to the stone images. It meant praying with candles, liquor, flowers, pine needles, incense, and contrition in one's heart.

Isabel decided that he did mean her mother. "She is too ill to come."

Eziquel looked Isabel up and down, measuring this suddenly strong voice in front of him. "Has she done what I told her?"

"Everything."

"Hm." He cast another glance at the woman inside. "All right."

Isabel waited by the door as he swept the things on his short table into a leather pouch: a line of thumb-sized crystals and two handfuls of red *tz'ite* beans. He placed a hand on the woman's shoulder. She was so caught up in ardent prayer that she had been oblivious to them. Her whole body jumped when he touched her.

"Finish," he consoled. "I must leave."

Her face was a blank.

"The gods listen and watch even when I am not here."

"Thank you," she replied, although Isabel felt sure that he had meant it more as a warning not to disturb anything than as reassurance that she would be heard by divine forces.

He placed his small pouch into a knit bag that said *Chichicastenango,* then draped the larger bag down his back with the thin strap across his forehead in the manner of a tumpline. "Now," he proclaimed to Isabel, and proceeded ahead of her down the pathway.

The people in the village looked on as they walked. One or two called out their regards and best wishes for Manuela. Through it all, Don Eziquel seemed to pay no heed. He walked with single-minded attention to the paths. And he moved surprisingly fast for a man in his sixties. Isabel kept up, but not without moving as quickly as she would have with any of her young friends. No words passed between them. She followed at a respectful distance as they traveled through the center of town and down further by the lake, where a narrow lane twisted off to take them home.

Isabel entered first and held the door open for Eziquel. Manuela lay on the bed, panting and clutching herself. She seemed too tired to open her eyes.

"Are you all right?" Isabel asked.

"Perhaps this is worse than I thought," Eziquel said.

And instead of this frightening Isabel, it gave her an odd hope: Perhaps her mother was only so ill because the *sanjorín* had underestimated the illness. Now that he understood exactly what forces he was dealing with, he'd be able to cure it and end the drama.

Isabel stayed close to the old man when he sat on the edge of the *petate* sleeping mat. He put his hand to Manuela's face. She opened her eyes and smiled weakly.

"You have come," she said.

"I have come."

Manuela tried to affect a stern look at Isabel, but her genuine thankfulness showed through. "I told her I was all right."

"She is worse, Don Eziquel. Don't listen to her."

The *sanjorín* raised his eyebrows at the young and presumptuous girl.

Isabel glanced down at her hands; her fingers twisted the ends of the sleeping mat.

"Tell me," Eziquel said.

Manuela showed him her swollen ankles. "They are much worse at night. At night everything is worse. I can't breathe, and it feels like someone is pounding and clutching at my chest from inside. I get tired too soon, Don Eziquel. Much too soon."

"Pobrecita"—"poor you."

"Before, it was only during the day that I felt so bad." Manuela cast a quick glance at her daughter. She had been openly denying her illness for so long that now she felt as if she were revealing a terrible and shameful secret.

"Yes," he consoled, feeling around her ankles.

"But now during the day, I start coughing. I get dizzy. I can't lift what I must to run a house."

"*Pobrecita.*"

Isabel shifted close by her mother and took hold of her hand.

"Vomiting?"

"No."

"Do you have changes of color in urine or bowel movement?"

Manuela shook her head.

"Fever?"

"Only a little."

"Make *yerbabuena* tea," Eziquel told Isabel. "Fortunately, you have such a strong daughter to help you when you're ill."

He said this distractedly as he searched in his pouch and removed things, unaware that his words opened for Isabel the floodgate of her dread of never returning to school. The water jug in her hand felt as heavy as rock now. She would be doomed to care for her family until they all moved away or died. Even marriage would be postponed. She would have to fight off her desires much longer than she had intended. A favorite image of Lucas Choy came to her: his strong, shirtless back bending to some task, his face suddenly turning sideways to look up at her and the light snatching black obsidian from his eyes. She conjured for herself his thin smile, with just the barest of white hinting at tremendous emotion beneath the casual surface. This passion had always been the hardest thing to keep at bay.

Her thoughts were erased by the *sanjorín* spreading

out his divining tools on the altar beside the stone image and by her mother saying, "Give him a chair."

But the old man already had his spotted fist around the wood. He waved her back. "Get the tea instead."

Isabel returned to blow the embers into flames. She added a few sticks, then arranged a pot of water on the metal disk. She dropped in mint leaves. From beside the fire, she watched Eziquel make a line of crystals on the shelf. In front of these, he piled his bright red *tz'ite* beans. He lit the four candles left always before the stone, then carried his incense pot to the fire. Isabel quickly scraped out coals for him, shoveling them into the pot with an ash scoop.

"We shall see," he whispered to her in such a private manner that he ignited her optimism all over again.

She looked across the room. Once more Manuela lay with her arms clutching her chest and her eyes pressed tightly together.

The *sanjorín* sprinkled yellow tree-sap incense over the coals and waved the smoking pot in each of the four directions. He recited in such a low voice that his words were unintelligible to Isabel or her mother. Then his right hand alternately stroked the crystals and a crucifix, while he asked loudly in Spanish that the celestial forces help Manuela, help her see what she must do and help her find a little peace in her poor life. "She is suffering," he prayed. "She is in pain. All she wants is a little guidance. Show her just a little of what is true."

"Please," Isabel whispered to herself.

Coxol again muttered in Tzutujil while grabbing and releasing handfuls of the beans. This time, his left hand stroked the crystals, and though Isabel heard the words

39

he said, she did not always understand them. Suddenly, sensing that the amount and the moment were correct, he did not drop his handful, but transferred them to the center of the shelf. These he arranged in two vertical lines of piles composed of four beans each. Two remaining beans were returned to the general pile. He counted up the left column and down the right, naming the ancient days—some of which Isabel recognized. When he finished, an "oh" bubbled out from him.

Isabel jerked forward so quickly that she nearly knocked over the pot of tea. The water hissed loudly as it lapped the hot metal sides of the pot.

Eziquel gathered the beans back into the large pile and once more prayed softly while he stroked the crystals and palmed the beans. Isabel felt her breath stop in her lungs. Coxol intuited again the amount to keep. He spread the beans into new columns: eight in the left, six in the right.

"Fourteen," he said.

"What?" Isabel asked. "What?"

Manuela perked up, too. "What is it, Don Eziquel?"

He shook his head and answered not Manuela, but Isabel.

She leaned forward, watching, trying to read the face behind his words.

"She is crying, suffering a great deal."

Manuela propped herself on one elbow.

"It is old and complicated. Something is severe. They are punishing."

"Punishing?"

Then he turned to Manuela. "Come here."

She painfully lifted herself from the floor and inched toward the altar.

"Punishing?" Isabel repeated, her body drawn forward by her need to know. "Why?"

However, Eziquel now paid no attention to her. He removed a thick knife from his knitted pouch and sent a chill into Isabel's spine.

Manuela knelt obediently beside the *sanjorín.*

"Is she . . . ?" Isabel felt her throat harden to stone as her mother looked across at her. All of them knew her question, but to ask it would give the possibility of Manuela's dying greater strength. To say something always made what was said more real, more possible.

"Give me your hand," Eziquel commanded.

Isabel saw, as for the first time, the weakness in her mother's joints, the fatigue in her eyes, all the swelling and evident pain she had been suffering for days and weeks. Isabel felt deeply ashamed for her selfish concerns. It was her own mother suffering, not some stranger: she who had suffered through the loss of two children, she who had no doubt suffered many other things as well.

Manuela reached her right hand out to the healer.

Both mother and daughter waited for the terrible diagnosis.

Eziquel stroked Manuela's arm as if it were the arm of a child or as if he meant to discover the language of comfort hidden beneath the flesh. Casually, his rheumy eyes fixed on her. "You will not die," he said.

For Isabel, a great flutter of wings carried that message. The quetzal wings lifted her up out of the squalor of the hut and high above the village, where she looked down upon the whole bowl of the lake, the volcano-ringed water, and farther—to the horizons, where she momentarily saw herself as another person going out, far out, into the world.

"If," Eziquel sliced in, "you make atonements."

Isabel saw the fog of disillusionment drape her, masking sounds and sights the way the morning fog deadened everything. She thought for a second that she heard animals running, clopping around rocks, scampering up to flee to the false safety of Oro Hill, but she realized it was none of that, only the hard boil of the *yerbabuena* tea beside her.

Don Eziquel opened his large bag again and withdrew a thin jade lancet and cup. Simultaneously, Isabel fished the pot from the flames. The *sanjorín* fully extended Manuela's arm over his knee. Isabel watched with fascination and fear, carelessly splashing a searing drop of water onto her fingers. Eziquel passed the lancet four times over the incense. Isabel drew a ceramic teacup toward her. She bit her tongue as the healer showed Manuela the spot on her arm where the tip was to be inserted. Eziquel prayed in a mixture of Spanish and Tzutujil. Isabel turned away and hurriedly poured the tea into the cup. Manuela's voice joined in traditional prayers and new prayers, spoken in earnest worship. Isabel anxiously moved forward, bringing the *yerbabuena* tea to the *sanjorín*.

And then the blade tip entered her mother's flesh.

"Oof" was all Manuela uttered, her head lolling to one side.

Isabel clamped a hand over her mouth; the tea splashed again.

A line of blood appeared and grew to a semicircle. Eziquel withdrew the point. Instantly, the blood ran thick. Eziquel moved his small cup to catch the flow and both of them prayed loudly. They forgot Isabel, who sat close enough to smell the metallic odor of blood mingling intoxicatingly with the sap incense and tarrow candles and the mint tea in her hand. Manuela nodded as she prayed. Her upper body rocked forward and back in anxious bowings. Eziquel stroked Manuela's back several times, as if to set the appropriate rhythm of the devotion. Once it was set, he motioned for Isabel to put down the tea.

Finally, with Manuela nearly collapsing from the strain, from the entrancing rocking and loss of blood, the *sanjorín* took Manuela's fingers and pressed them tightly against the wound to stop the flow.

"Now," he said. "You must feed every day." He poured the blood from his cup into the stone's circular mouth. The blood overflowed to run dark around the natural rock cuts that formed the lips and chin, and down further in a red fall to the ground.

Manuela swayed dangerously backward.

"Mami!" Isabel said, lunging to catch her.

"I'm all right," she began, but she saw in her daughter's face something afraid, something penned inside that demanded the dark truth from her. "Oh, *hijita*, I'm not all right." She stroked Isabel's face. "I'm not all right at all."

Isabel pressed her eyes closed.

Eziquel prayed a moment longer, oblivious to the women. He dug into the ground by the altar with the large knife, then scraped and scooped out the dirt until

43

he had made a hole the size of his fist. "Watch," he said. He first cleaned the hole of loose dirt, then scraped a second hole into the side wall. "This hole is to save you." He brought out in his clenched hand the dirt from the side hole and rubbed it over Manuela's wound. "Every day," he prescribed again. The blood and dirt coagulated into a muddy patch. Manuela nodded grimly, trying bravely to keep her attention from leaking away like her blood. She slumped, but instantly straightened to await what other sacrifices she would have to make.

"Now the tea," Eziquel ordered.

Isabel held out the cup in quivering hands, her own mind nearly numb with questions, with fears, with expectations of worse things to come.

They watched as Don Eziquel grasped the cup of steaming tea with both hands and brought it slowly to his pursed lips.

Five

That night, Alfredo Pacay came home with a lashing of wood more than a meter in diameter in his tumpline. José rushed to help him lower the heavy load. Alfredo wiped his brow with the old cloth he'd used to protect his back. Together, the two of them pulled the stack toward the rear of the hut. José started to drag it to the family pile.

"No," Alfredo said. "This is to sell." He threw the cloth over the wood.

José was more than happy to leave the wood where it lay and to get to more important business. "Did you hear about the American?"

Alfredo nodded grimly and led them into the house. Inside, Isabel sat hunched by the fire as she made tortillas. Marcelina sat beside her sister and used an old cob and her fingers to scrape corn from a heap of cobs in a basket between her legs. Both paused and looked up at their father. He walked directly back to Manuela without a word, leaving the girls quietly struggling to hear their parents' muffled conversation behind the blanket partition.

José slumped down by a wall and poked the hard ground with a stick. "Did you see the American?" he asked Isabel.

"Sh." She scooted closer to the blanket.

"I did!" Marcelina said, her eyes full of wonder.

"Sh!"

José sneered at Isabel and continued as loudly as before. "He's tall, isn't he?"

"And ugly," Marcelina said happily.

"Ugly?" Isabel asked in surprise. "Why do you say that?"

"You don't think so?"

"I don't know."

"All foreigners are ugly. They're fat."

"He wasn't fat."

José laughed at their argument. "And noisy." He perched his hands atop the stick. "And arrogant."

"All right!" Isabel said.

"And too big," Marcelina continued.

"And too white," José added.

"They look sick."

"Stop it!"

Suddenly the blanket swooshed out.

Alfredo glared at them. "What's the matter?" His eyes dared a response. "Don't make so much noise. Your mother needs to rest."

José and Marcelina's teasing died away in soft chuckles.

"Never mind about the American!" Alfredo said. "They're only trouble."

46

"That's not what he said this morning."

Alfredo stared at Isabel. "And who are you to believe: your father or that stranger?"

Marcelina smiled sheepishly. "She thinks he's handsome—"

"I do not!"

"Yes, you do; yes, you do—"

"Enough!" Alfredo pushed the long tail of his belt under him and sat at the doorway. "As if there aren't enough troubles."

The children ended their play.

Alfredo gazed out across the lake. From their doorway, the great tourist town of Panajachel was just visible. During the day, when it was clear, the abandoned hotel towers stood incomplete and gray, testimony to the great wasteful wealth located like a vicious tease within sight. At night, before any fogbanks interceded, hundreds of electric lights could be seen flickering across the water. To the left and right of that modern world, small villages were distinguishable by their only available lighting: the faint and reddish glimmer of firelight.

Alfredo turned back to those inside. "Where's Diego?"

"Playing with his top." José stood when he saw that his father meant something more. "I'll get him."

Alfredo let his older son squeeze past; then he turned to Isabel. "And dinner?"

She had stacked some twenty tortillas in her shoulder scarf to keep them warm and was stirring a simmering pot of black beans. "Ready."

"Marcelina," he said, digging out money from plastic wrap he had hidden in the folds of his belt. He handed her two half-quetzal notes and ten centavos.

47

Marcelina ran down the path toward the home of Reanda Tziná to buy her father a half pint of Venado. It amounted to a sixth of his daily earnings, but it was the only luxury their father had. He did not even own leather sandals or tennis shoes, like many of the men. He would never in his life own boots like the store owners or fine shoes like the ladinos. Someday he might be able to throw away the rubber sandals for leather ones, but with payments to the *sanjorín* and the few quetzales per month for education, it seemed like something that would come only with divine fortune. None of the family begrudged him his one treat of rum. In fact, with drink, Alfredo slipped into stories that entertained them all.

Isabel scooped beans into shallow bowls and set them on the floor. She placed the stack of tortillas in the center, then brought forth a handful of scalding peppers, made even hotter by planting them while smoking a smelly cigar.

Diego came in ahead of José. He wound a string around his wooden top, then he affectionately slapped at Isabel's skirt before sitting down to eat. Alfredo sat against the wall, with José beside him. The males began without waiting for Marcelina, so Isabel stood watching by the door for her little sister.

Alfredo called to her. "Give your mother food." He held the bowl up for her to fill. She placed a few tortillas on top.

Manuela had her eyes closed.

"Mami?" Isabel whispered. Her mother didn't move, and for a terrible second, Isabel thought she was dead. "Mami!"

Manuela snorted and turned her face.

Isabel rubbed her eyes with her free hand to erase the sudden horror that had leaped into her head.

Alfredo's voice broke over the partition. "Leave her alone if she's sleeping. Watch for your sister."

Isabel again stood by the door. The males of the family leaned against the walls and used tortillas to spoon the beans. Alfredo ate a pepper with nearly every tortilla. José could only eat two of the chiles, and Diego didn't dare eat even one. Females would never be expected to eat peppers.

Alfredo and his sons were nearly finished by the time Marcelina appeared. The two girls quickly joined the others and began to eat. Just as Isabel had her first mouthful, Alfredo told her to pick a lime from one of the trees and to bring him salt. José asked for water, followed by Diego. Marcelina asked, too.

Alfredo twisted off the seal of the rum, pinched some salt onto his tongue, and gulped the whole bottle in one draught. His face screwed into a grimace as he reached for a slice of lime. Fascinated, the boys watched with little comprehension as to why their father would drink something that so obviously tasted bad.

Diego put the bottle to his nose. "Brr," he said, shaking the stink from his head.

Alfredo laughed. "Finally," he said, "this too is from the ladino. Perhaps from foreigners. Who knows? Our ancestors drank only for ceremonies, something made with honey and nance-fruit."

The boys had finished, but Isabel and Marcelina ate with their heads close to the bowls and looking up at their father. Alfredo leaned back comfortably. He stared out the open door, into the darkness settling decisively on the village. Only two oil lamps and the embers of the fire lit the square room. His face was cast in shifting shadows. At times it seemed his eyes were closed; then a patch of light sprang from his dark pupils, as the strong drink seeped into the tributaries of his body.

"It is like smoking. Before it was only for ceremonies. Now there are those who smoke all day long. And in the east, tobacco companies offer so much to the farmers that they turn away from growing food and grow only poison. It's like I always say: So much is gone." He passed a hand through his hair. "Unless you remember." He smiled directly at Isabel. "Even when you learn about the rest of the world, it's good to remember what has come before."

José drew closer to his father. It was common for Alfredo to tell them stories at night or to teach them or to chastise in the manner of a lesson. He did this just before going to sleep, just after the sun dropped behind San Pedro, when their small home seemed safe and good and full of uncomplicated affection.

"Yes," he said, deciding on what he would say. "Even this American." He shifted his weight. "I tell you, long ago, the twelve *naguales* lived around here. You don't know this, but some of the old ones say they were boys when the *naguales* lived around here and in Santiago Atitlán. Others say that it was long before, during the time of our ancient city, Oro Hill. But before, when everyone traveled to Mazatenango to sell, they traveled the roads and went to sleep in the city, but there was this powerful dog, a magic dog. They say that it was a man. It smoked cigars and drank. It wore pants. It was the government's dog.

"Our people went and stayed in a large room in Mazate. But the government dog was powerful, magical.

50

Who knows what kind of magic it had, but nothing would kill it. Not machetes, not knives—nothing would harm it. The people slept in the room, and then the dog entered. It put its burning cigar on the bottom of their feet and killed people. The magic did it. The power of the dog killed them. The dead people never came back to their homes in Santiago or Chuuí Chopaló. Instead, the dog ordered the government horses to carry the corpses back. These horses carried the bodies, the dead ones, back to the government.''

Alfredo faced Marcelina to get the desired effect: "The government sold the bodies to the United States for food!"

Marcelina cowered into Isabel's side.

Alfredo smiled. "Well, the *naguales* met and discussed why people would not return from Mazate. Why they disappeared after going down the roads. The *naguales* used their powers of divination. 'Let us discover what this is,' they said to one another, and they found out it was the government dog. But what force that dog had! Nothing killed it. People fought with machetes, with everything! But nothing killed it. So the *naguales* went and battled against it and understood the magic that this animal had.

"See, the dog was very powerful, very strong. Ver-ry magical! But the *naguales* were great wizards. Just as we speak to one another and understand one another, they understood all things. Everything was clear to them. Nothing was hidden from them.

"The *naguales* used beans to divine. One said, 'You turn into an eagle, and I will fight the dog. You fly up as an eagle; I will have this stone.' It was a stone about this big.'' Alfredo touched his thumb and middle finger together.

51

"They went to Mazate and pretended to sleep, these *naguales*. They stretched out and closed their eyes. The dog came in. It was wearing heavy metal armor, like the Spanish warriors. It was ferocious. Nothing would kill it. The *naguales* fought with machetes, with knives, but the animal was too powerful. The one *nagual* became an eagle. The *naguales* attacked the dog three times. One *nagual* fought very hard. Suddenly, the eagle came down and grabbed the dog, lifting it all the way to the middle of heaven. Another *nagual* threw the stone. It was a little stone, about this big, but it grew after he threw it. The stone became very large and flat, and the eagle let the dog fall. That dog dropped from the middle of heaven and smashed against the stone. The metal armor shattered, and that ended the terrible dog, the government dog.

"The *naguales* knew everything. They knew how to speak to animals. They put the corpse of the dog on the horses and said, 'Send this to your masters. Let this be their meat.' Then they went hurrying down the pathways, down the roads and along the hills, back to Atitlán.

"When the government saw the dog, they were angry. What kind of magician could kill their magic dog? 'It must be someone very strong, very powerful,' they said. 'We must find out who did this.' They sent the army here. The army entered Santiago and walked among the villages of the lake. But the *naguales* had already come back. They had walked quickly along the roads, not slowly like the ladino. The army asked everyone, 'Who killed the government dog? Who did this?' No one knew anything. They told the army that they did not know who did it. 'It must be someone

52

really strong,' our people said, but that is all. 'We know nothing,' they said. 'We can tell you nothing.' "

José smiled hugely.

"Some of the old ones say the *naguales* are coming back right now. They are on their way because we are in trouble again."

Diego was hooked. "Really?"

"Some say they are coming from the States. They are driving a Chevrolet right now to get here."

All of the children's eyes opened wide.

"When they arrive, one will speak Tzutujil. He will be powerful. He won't be like these other foreigners, who only speak Spanish and want to buy clothes. He will know our customs. He will respect our secrets."

Alfredo peered at them. "He will speak Tzutujil. And he will be very, ver-ry strong."

Later that night, Isabel fell asleep listening to a squirrel pack new thatch into its nest among the crannies of their ceiling. Her mind wandered all over her father's story. For a moment, she played with the idea that the American in the clearing was a *nagual,* yet he barely spoke Spanish and he knew even less of their language or of their world. She realized that the story, in part, was to show why no one in the villages ever revealed anything of consequence when people were killed or when they disappeared forever. No one was ever captured, no one was ever sent to jail, when these horrible things happened. And no one ever knew who had committed the murders. That was what their father meant to convey in telling the story, because of their silly chattering about the American.

The scratching and scurrying of the squirrel sounded like a gentle and intermittent rain on the thatch roof.

53

Isabel dozed off and on with the curiously restful sound, while grappling with the puzzles of three attacks on the dog, the suit of armor, and the Americans who ate the flesh of the Maya. Her teacher, Andrés Xiloj, certainly never spoke about the Americans in that way. It was such a strange story, with these both demonic and majestic Americans. And that paradoxical thought wound its serpentine way through the deep underbrush of her unconscious, the stones and obstacles of her conscious mind, until she finally dozed off.

Teresa called at the fence one day at one o'clock, when school ended and students went home to eat and rest a bit before going to the family fields or doing errands. Teresa called out for Isabel, her forearms draped over the uneven points of the upright cornstalks.

Isabel hurried excitedly out of the house.

Teresa stood smiling, her teeth sparkling with the two silver stars. "My mother wants me to tell you that when her sister had chest pains the *sanjorín* told her to spread pork lard on her chest, and mustard leaves front and back, and wrap it all with a clean white cloth. Do this for three days just before going to sleep. It cured my aunt."

"Tell your mother that we all thank her."

Teresa grasped Isabel's hand with her two hands. "How is she?"

"She tries working every morning, but she doesn't sleep at night and she can't work for long."

"That's too bad."

"She says she feels her heart fighting all night long. She says she can't breathe. So in the morning she's too tired to do much."

"She must be suffering."

"She still wants to work."

"Well, that's something."

"Yes. But I do it all." Isabel quickly swung the front end of her shawl to the other shoulder and covered her mouth with it. She glanced back at the door. "Well, how's Maestro Xiloj?"

"Tsk. Are you never coming back?"

"Don't ask," she said through the cloth.

"The teachers ask. Everyone wonders."

"Oh, Teresa, I want to go back." Again she muffled her words with the shawl. "I hate being here. When she sleeps, I don't do anything. But I have to stay and help. I have to."

"I know."

"I'm kept in and I'm never going to learn another thing. I'm never going to know anything."

Teresa shrugged. "What do girls need to know, anyway?"

Isabel drooped onto the fence with a deep sigh. "You know what I mean."

"Come on, you'll be married soon."

Isabel caught Teresa's starry smile. She was beautiful, prettier after the dentist had inserted the stars. But to Isabel, her true beauty was in continuing her friendship with Isabel even after the marriage her family had planned for her with Lucas ended when Lucas fell in love with Isabel. She had said that it was her parents' plan, not hers. And, as if to prove it, Teresa eagerly helped Isabel communicate with Lucas, helped her know what a girl should and should not do with a boy. There was nothing Isabel did not tell her friend, nothing they did not share.

"You know," Isabel answered, "that I haven't seen Lucas for days now. Not really, anyway. Just once when the American was here."

Teresa sympathetically squeezed her hand. "Did he ask you to marry him again?"

"The American?"

Teresa laughed. "Don't be silly!"

Isabel blushed. "No, the last time he just stood there."

"Oh?"

"He's angry about something."

"Are you sure?"

"I don't know why he should be angry."

"He's a man. That's why."

They watched boys play marbles a short distance down the path. The boys shuffled on their haunches to aim their shots.

Isabel slipped her hands into Teresa's. "Are you going home?"

Teresa nodded.

"Will you see Lucas?"

"No."

"Have you seen him, then?"

Teresa shifted uncomfortably. "Yes."

"Well?"

"What?"

"Did he say anything?"

"Like what?"

"Teresa!"

She pulled her hands back and folded them into her shawl. "Not really," she said.

"What did he say?"

56

"Nothing, really." Teresa carefully adjusted her scarf so that it hung the proper way: over her shoulder, the ends even in front and back and hanging below her waist. Hers was a dark green-blue with fine silver threading, much newer than Isabel's.

"You're hiding something."

"Why do you say that?"

Isabel felt like screaming. "Stop it!" she growled.

"Nothing," Teresa said, fidgeting with the knot of hair at the base of her skull. "Really."

Isabel glowered.

"Well," she conceded, "he does wonder why you haven't seen him."

"What?"

"I told him, 'Don't you know her mother's sick?' "

"What is he thinking? How can he think such a thing?"

"I told him he should respect a girl who cares for her family above all others, even above her fiancé."

"But I want to see him!" Isabel pulled the shawl tightly around her shoulders. "I *would* see him . . . if I could. How can I see him? And when?"

"I don't know."

"Tell him, Teresa."

"Of course I will."

"You'll tell him that I miss him."

"Yes, of course."

Isabel looked down the path. "What is he thinking?"

They watched the marble-playing boys drift off to their homes with rambunctious jostling and laughter.

"Anyway," Isabel said, trying on a cloak of irritation, "why hasn't he come here? Why hasn't he shown my family respect?"

Teresa pulled her shawl across her breasts. "I don't know."

They looked at each other without a word until Isabel's affected irritation felt natural and real, justified, not just pretended. "Anyway," she said, "he's committed himself."

Teresa raised her eyebrows in shock.

"He said he loved me."

"Oh," Teresa said in relief.

Isabel settled the shawl decisively over her shoulders.

"That does mean something," said Teresa.

Isabel nodded.

There was nothing more to say, it seemed. Teresa moved to leave. "Don't worry. I'll talk to him."

Isabel smiled.

"I'll talk to him, Isabel. Really."

Up the road from the lake, men dipped and rose to their hard labor. One long scar puckered on the ground from just above the lake, near where the women washed clothes, to fifty yards up, where a gang, including Lucas Choy, hoed and shoveled the waterline channel. Isabel walked slowly up the incline, keeping her eye on Lucas's back as it broadened when he bent and leaped into brilliant muscle lines when he lifted out earth. His body shimmered with sweat. Because of her single-minded attention to him, she nearly stumbled on a sleeping dog by a trash heap. The emaciated animal yelped and scampered away, hipbones protruding, a wound festering where someone had landed a stone. The only real flesh on the poor dog was her pathetically inadequate teats. This was a mother with starving pups.

The men joked loudly as they worked, making fun of one another and challenging one another to work faster. No one noticed Isabel until she was nearly upon them.

"Lucas," one of the men called. He pointed back with a twist of his chin.

Lucas dumped his shovel-load atop the scar that swelled foot by foot toward the center of town. He peered up, one eye closed against the sun.

"Hello," Isabel said.

He nodded.

"Hello!" she said again, head cocked forward, her body angling away from the others.

He forced a mumbled "Hi."

Isabel walked to the other side of the avenue, setting a gaff into him with a sidelong glance that concealed none of her irritation.

He climbed stiffly out of the channel and obediently followed her to the shade.

"What's the matter?" she said so the others would not hear.

Lucas looked back at those still working. "What's the matter with you?"

Isabel's arms were hidden under her shawl, now draped modestly in front. She did not answer, but let her silence weigh heavily enough to place the responsibility of an answer with him.

He moved his toe in short jabs against the ground.

The silence became tangible and awkward between them.

Finally he broke. "You've been gone for days."

"My mother's sick," she answered quickly. "You know that."

Lucas bobbed his head as if to discover in the air something more persuasive to say.

Isabel took the offensive: "Your own mother came a week ago."

Lucas winced.

"*You* haven't."

"I've been working every day. First in the field and now with putting the pipe in for water." He tried distracting her with a large smile: "We expect to have the pump and faucet in a week."

"Ah-hum."

"Well, it is important." He looked at the ground. "And it's hard work."

Isabel softened under his boyish defense. "I know, Lucas. I do."

Neither looked at the other, staring instead at the earth between them.

Their silence nurtured in him a desire to touch her, to stroke the hair from her face. "How is your mother, anyway?"

Isabel sighed. "Worse."

"I'm sorry."

His eyes were like black obsidian, with just the faintest of jade flecks. Isabel looked behind him at the distant mountain ridges. This new silence had become a lightness that slowly eroded the hard points of her anger, the way the wind rounds out rocks and stony crags.

"I miss you," she whispered, looking down at his blunt fingers, her words like a sigh from her.

But suddenly, a loud clang and shout from the others

broke through. Both turned to see the men roaring over a snake one of them had smashed with a shovel. The head was pulp and gore. The body writhed and coiled around the gruesome center, pasted by blood and flesh to the narrow path. The men watched the grotesque whirligig of dying flesh. Finally, by twists, the body separated from the head and, like a spring, it coiled down the incline. The workers were ecstatic. One of them lifted the body with his machete and held it out for inspection. Lucas waved that he could see it. The youngest boys were shocked at the iridescent corpse; the older men tried to guess what kind of snake it was. "Masaquat," one decided, and heaved the corpse into the air. The ropelike body arced into light, flashing for a moment as if it would come to life and fly away, then dropped to its rightful ground with a puff of straw flecks and dust. The workers took the opportunity to break and argue in a more leisurely way exactly what kind of snake it surely was.

Isabel gently tugged at Lucas's elbow, bringing his attention back to her, to her last words, to them and not some snake. She saw him struggling to remember what it was she had last said.

Finally, he knew. "I miss you, too."

"Well, that doesn't sound like you mean it."

He squirmed. "Sure I do. I mean it." But then he drew himself up defensively. "What about you?"

"Yes."

"More than school?"

"Of course."

He scoffed. "It's hard to believe."

Isabel wrapped herself in her scarf.

"I hear that you think more about school than about your own mother."

"That's not fair!"

"A girl should take care of her family, you know."

"That's what I'm doing."

He pointed an accusatory finger: "Without selfish feelings?"

Isabel could not help but blush.

"If this is the way you feel now, what will happen later?"

"What do you mean?"

"When you get married."

"What do—" And then she saw his brooding look, his concern, and it all became perfectly clear to her. "This is what you've been angry about, isn't it? This is why you've been distant. Isn't it?"

"What am I supposed to think?"

"I'm taking care of my mother. And the family."

"And you don't want to go back to school?"

She could not lie.

"You don't complain about having to take care of the family?"

"This isn't fair, Lucas."

His voice got loud enough to make the others turn. "What am I supposed to think? What kind of woman acts like that?"

She spoke quietly, desperately. "This is what you think?"

"Well?" he demanded.

She could only repeat herself impotently. "You think this?"

Lucas let the silence work its way into her.

She found no words. In her heart she was too confused to think, too unsure of her own motives and feelings to know what to say even quietly, within herself. Instead, she could only repeat her pathetic defense: "This is what you think?" Her voice held no conviction, only the tinniness of repetition.

Lucas stared at Isabel as if realizing something he had previously only been suspecting. The air became hard and crisp.

"Yes," he said in a horrible voice. "This is what I think."

She could not speak, even as he turned and walked back to the others. She stood transfixed by her own confusion and doubt. She *had* been complaining. Maybe she was selfish. Maybe teaching was a preposterous goal. Maybe she wasn't good enough for him. Maybe he should have remained faithful to Teresa and to the plans of her family.

Lucas glanced at Isabel before leaping, feet together, into the channel. The others shifted to allow Lucas room among them, and then they all stared back at her.

Maybe she was completely and totally wrong in this.

Six

Isabel chatted at the water's edge with Helisabet, Rosario, and Catarina, all married women her age—two already with children. Catarina had married a man fifteen years older than she when she was only fourteen. The others had married men their age. All of them teased Isabel, taunting her with questions as to why she was waiting so long to marry, how she could be happy living with her family and not a husband, and why she didn't go beyond just *thinking* of having children.

"Become a woman," they urged.

Isabel knew that in this case, it was meant lightheartedly more than seriously. It was common enough for girls to marry young, under pressure to leave the house—after all, a girl was more burden than asset until she became a woman, or so the traditional view went—but these women were just having a little fun with her.

They were voicing everyone's opinion, but in a good-natured way.

She rinsed her family's clothes beside one of the many flat rocks that formed a line in the water. Older women washed further away, so that these four were side by side. Each had an orange ball of soap that spread faint rainbow trails of oils on the surface of the water. The others had just started their wash, but Isabel twisted her washing one final time to squeeze out the water, then removed her blouse and rolled her skirt to just above her knees. She bathed with the laundry soap.

"She seems to be getting younger," Catarina teased.

The other two laughed.

"Yes," Helisabet added, "most girls get older, but this one seems only to stay the same."

Her head full of lather, Isabel smiled at their mannered speech.

"Perhaps she doesn't know what fun it is to be married?"

"Tell her, Rosario!" Helisabet said, punctuating with a hard *thwack* of pants against rock. Bubbles foamed out from the cotton.

"Where should I begin?"

"There's endless pleasure."

Catarina struck a pose and pretended to think: "Well, she knows about washing clothes."

Rosario agreed. "And she knows about cooking."

"Surely she knows about working from dawn to past dusk when the men are asleep."

"And she knows about taking care of children," Helisabet added.

The three smiled conspiratorially.

"But is it worth it?" Rosario questioned.

"Oh, yes, yes!" the other two chimed. All three broke into peals of laughter.

Isabel dunked her head, then twisted her hair as she had twisted the clothes to get rid of soap and water. "Why should I want the pain of childbirth?"

"Pain?" Rosario said in mock surprise. "The pleasure!"

"And why should I hurry the constant demands of a husband?"

"Demands? Oh, no, not demands. Needs and affection."

"They're like children," Catarina explained.

"They need our help."

"Of course," Isabel said. "Children that poke and prod far more than any little one!"

Again, the three women exploded into laughter.

Isabel combed through her long, thick hair. "No, I think I'll stay a girl for a little while longer." She put on her blouse and folded the clothes into her basket. "Give my best to your mothers-in-law," she said with a wink, then walked proudly up the path.

The three friends laughed happily behind her.

At home, Isabel unfolded the clothes and spread them along the fence. She watched a small sparrow drop a yellowish nut from a tree in an effort to crack the shell. The poor bird battled vainly against the tough hull and against the grounded chickens that scrambled to steal the food each time it was dropped. The sparrow always snatched the nut from the hens, but the main problem was that the hull would not crack. The bird tried the whole time Isabel hung clothes to dry. Finally it gave up and carried the nut way over the trees to some distant place. Isabel watched the bird until it disappeared.

The pig pushed its snout against Isabel's leg, and she remembered that she had not yet fed the animals. She went inside to get the sack of feed hanging on a nail by the door, then returned to spread the grain in an arc before the chickens and the pig.

As she did this, she heard someone saying hello. She turned to see the tall American waiting by the gate.

"I'm Allan Waters," he said, "and I—"

"¿Cómo?"

"Allan Waters."

"Ah-LANE Gwah-TARES?"

"AL-len WAH-turs."

"Oh. Ah-LANE Gwah-TARES."

"Well . . . yes, why not?"

Isabel noticed his small teeth when he smiled.

"And what's your name?"

"Isabel."

He lifted up his clipboard and clicked a silver pen. "What is your full name?"

Isabel shook her head.

"Okay. Isabel."

As he wrote, he held his mouth down to one side as if he were nipping the inside of his mouth with the points of his canine teeth.

"How old are you?"

Isabel stared back.

"Okey doke." He scratched something else on his paper.

Isabel watched his mouth work its inside flesh as he

67

wrote. She wondered if his little rodent teeth would nibble through his chin.

"Are you the mother of the house?"

Isabel noticed the backpack straps around his shoulders and looked behind him. It was a leather pack, partly opened, with a white drawstring hanging down to another pocket. "How much did that cost?" she asked.

Allan Waters took it off and handed it to her. It was heavy.

"Twenty-five dollars. Let's see: about sixty-five quetzales."

"Sixty-five!" She looked at his tennis shoes, his collared shirt and blue jeans. He had a silver watch on his left wrist. She opened his pack and pulled out a camera.

"Wait!" he yelped and took the camera from her.

"How much did that cost?"

"I don't know. Maybe five, six hundred—"

"Dollars?"

"Quetzales. May I take a picture?"

"No." She shrank back, her arms holding out the pack as a shield.

"Thank you." He inserted the camera and threaded his arms through the straps.

Isabel stared up at him. She could not guess his age. He seemed, by his foreignness—his blond, curly hair; his great height, which seemed to want more and more of the sky; his blue, shallow eyes—to be a full-grown man; yet there was something about his clean-shaven face and soft skin that made her sure he was still a young man, perhaps Lucas's age.

"Listen," he said, "I'm here in Chuuí Chopaló to—"

68

"*¿Cómo?*"

"I'm here in Chuuí Chopaló . . ." he said slowly, pronouncing slowly.

"Yes," she answered, "this is Chuuí Chopaló."

He laughed. "My Spanish is not very good."

"No. It is very good. Perfect, in fact."

He shifted the backpack on his shoulders. "You're very kind."

"How did you get here?"

"Here or in Guatemala?"

"Yes."

He chuckled at how she turned the question into a yes/no question. He opted for the general location. "I flew."

"In a plane?" Isabel was sure that each time this strange man opened his mouth some new wonder would spill out between those small, inadequate teeth.

"Of course."

She looked up into the sky. "How much did it cost?"

He leaned forward, full of suspicions. "Why do you want to know how much everything costs?"

Isabel waited patiently for an answer.

Allan gave up and figured in his head, his mouth working again. "About one thousand five hundred quetzales."

The amount knocked loose a gasp from Isabel.

"Less, maybe." The shock on her face frightened him, made him see all chance of truly connecting slip away. "Maybe less, I think. Yes, it was less. Much less, now that I think about it. It was little. I can't remember how much, but it was much, much less. Hardly anything at all, it was so little."

69

"Dios mío!"

"But listen," he evaded, "I came to talk to you about something else. Something that I can help with." He waited for her attention to come back from the vault of the sky that allowed for such things as airplanes and two years' salary to be spent so quickly. "I'm here doing an investigation for medicine."

"Help?" she asked from her daze.

"Yes. I'm doing an investigation for medicine."

Isabel focused away from imagined airplanes. "I don't understand." And an image of her mother began slowly to form.

"Well, people have illnesses and they can't explain it to a doctor—"

"Why did you come here?" she blurted, suddenly in fear and awe that he would know about her mother or know anything about the family. Her father's story of the *naguales* instantly came back, as did the talk of politics.

Allan shrugged. "I've tried other houses. You're the only one who's listened even this much."

Isabel again saw the boyishness of his face, saw something young in his frustration.

"Please," he said.

She did not move.

"I'm trying to draw pictures that show . . . *symptomos*. No, *síntomes*—for illnesses. Do you understand?"

Isabel stared blankly.

"Do you understand? Well, people who are sick have symptoms that they may not be able to explain to a doctor because they only speak Mayan. If I can draw pictures that show symptoms—so they make sense without the person having to know Spanish or Tzutujil or Cakchiquel—people can use the pictures to point out what's wrong so the doctor understands. People will get help without having to find translators. They can go directly to the doctor. See? There won't be misunderstandings. It's perfect for a place like Guatemala, which has so many different languages," Allan Waters finished proudly. "In this way, the ill person can speak directly to the doctor. It's my idea."

Isabel rubbed her brow. "What doctor?"

"Any doctor. It doesn't matter."

"Don Coxol?"

"Well, yes." Allan smiled. "Who's he?"

"He speaks Tzutujil."

"Another doctor, then. It doesn't matter."

Isabel tried to see past the American's blue eyes to something that made sense, something deeper. "Why are you here?"

"Do you mean why do I have to come here and not just make the pictures with the doctor?"

"Yes. Why are you here?"

"Well, to learn what sorts of pictures make sense. To see what cultural things might affect the way I make the pictures."

Isabel's mother shouted for her. She turned from the fence to see her mother at the door. Manuela waved her arm angrily and spoke rapidly in Tzutujil, then disappeared inside as suddenly as she had appeared.

"What did she say?"

Isabel would not look him in the face. "I have to go."

"Is that your mother?"

71

"Yes."

"Can I speak with her?"

"No!"

"What did she say?"

Isabel looked up. "She said 'who are you to come here and speak to me?' "

"But I'm only trying to help."

Isabel shrugged. "Who asked you?"

"No one asked me; I applied for—" He stopped himself as he suddenly understood: No one at all had asked him. He had come on his own, with his own ideas, to save these "poor, unfortunate" people. He stared helplessly at Isabel.

"I'm sorry," she said. She squeezed through the gate and past him to the narrow path. "I have to go."

Seven

sabel walked to the center of the village to buy her mother mineral-lime from Mauricio Chevajay. She knew it was not a real errand—after all, wasn't she now the one who kept track of what was needed in the house?—but a way to get her away from the American poking around where he shouldn't be poking, expecting things answered as if he were "someone from the military," as her mother had snarled from the doorway. Isabel's mind still echoed with her mother's final attack: "And whose military is he with?"

It was unfair, Isabel thought, though understandable. Her mother had not heard a word that had gone between them. To her, what passed between Isabel and Allan Waters were questions, personal as all questions are, and the writing down of things. Both could only mean trouble. The exact words didn't need to be heard. The supposed reason didn't need to be listened to.

Isabel walked up by the men working in the new water trench. She approached and stared intently at Lucas's back until he felt her eyes boring into his flesh. When he turned, she smiled.

"Hello."

"Hello," he said warily.

She shuffled. "I'm on my way to the store."

"Ah," he said, his shovel snicking into the earth. He kept one foot propped on the blade; he waited.

Isabel turned a slow, appreciative gaze up and down the waterline. "It looks like it won't be long."

"A few more days."

She, however, didn't want rapid replies. She lingered over his words before answering. "That's good."

"Yes," he said and kicked the spade into the earth. "I'd better get back."

"But you look hot."

He shrugged.

"Should I bring you water?"

Lucas studied her. He seemed to think that her desire was formal, as if it did not spring from a genuine desire, but only a wish to ease things between them, not *deal* with things between them. It was not spontaneous, but calculated. And it was not at all what he wanted. "I'm fine," he answered.

She hid her hands in her shawl. *"Baik'a."* She said good-bye in a respectful way, the way one would to a stranger or superior.

On the return, she nodded hello from as far to the other side of the avenue as the narrow road would al-

74

low. He nodded quickly in return, his hands full of the shovel and heavy dirt.

Back home, she heard a great commotion inside. Several neighbor women were in the house, speaking excitedly with Manuela. When Isabel entered the door, the voices suddenly fell and all the faces turned to her. For an instant, the shadowed faces seemed grim and ghostly, like apparitions come to take her mother into the other world. But just as suddenly, the faces flicked away and their human chatter resumed. Isabel placed the lime into a wide-mouthed urn of milky water with other pieces of the stone, then squatted against the wall to listen. The neighbors encircled her mother, each woman pecking forward like a hen as she spoke, to ensure she was heard. Each woman pecked at the serious problem dropped before them all.

"He came yesterday," one woman named María said. "I didn't say a word to him, of course."

"Neither did I," Josefa said.

"Trouble."

"But *she* let him in," Rosa said.

"She should not have let him in," Josefa warned.

Isabel wondered which of the neighbor women had allowed Allan Waters into her home. These women would keep an eye on anyone doing such a thing. Who knew what witchcraft might ensue? Who knew how the village would respond?

"And we want to know what he said," María proclaimed.

"Trouble," a woman repeated. It was Catarina's mother.

Manuela sprawled on her mat, propped up on one

75

elbow to listen to the women. She moved her head sideways as each new speaker rocked forward to be heard.

"He stood with her for several minutes," said Rosa. "We watched him! Nothing good can come of this, Manuela. Nothing good."

Josefa leaned ominously forward: "And he wrote things down."

"Very bad!"

"Why did she let him in?"

Manuela threw up her arms. "I don't know."

And it was then that Isabel realized the women were speaking about her, not some other woman in the village.

"I didn't let him in," she protested. "He was outside the fence."

Manuela shushed her. "I sent her away," she said to the others.

"What did he say?" demanded Rosa. She turned for approval to two women who had been silent. They gave it with cluckings in their throats.

"And what did he write?" Josefa insisted.

"He asked her questions, so I sent her away."

Isabel felt a sliver of anger enter her: If they wanted to know what the American had said, they should ask her. Instead, they not only did not ask, but acted as if she were not there beside them.

"Why?—" she began.

"Sh!" Manuela said again.

"Trouble!" repeated Catarina's mother.

María bobbed forward: "Perhaps he's a spy?"

All the women hummed with that thought, their

heads jerking from side to side as they looked at one another, enthusiastic over this tantalizing idea.

"The army?" one questioned.

"Of the United States."

That generated a new flurry of "hums" and "tsks." Catarina suddenly saw the large picture: "The elections are coming."

"No, not for another year."

Josefa justified her friend's opinion: "They're already campaigning."

Most of them nodded at that sensible answer.

"With every election there are more and more deaths."

"It's too early."

"They're anxious to get started."

"Anxious for the killing, that is! That's why they want to begin so soon!"

"But he's too young," Isabel shouted.

They did not look at her, even though Josefa answered the charge. "That's merely a trick." They acted as if it had been posed by one of them.

"Who can tell how old these strangers are?" Rosa said.

Several answered, "I can't."

"They all look alike."

"He could be any age."

The discussion wound to a close. "One thing for sure: He must not come here again," Josefa warned.

The woman agreed among themselves, then proclaimed their public decision for Manuela: "He will not come here again."

Manuela assented. "No."

The women rose to leave, and it seemed to turn into any other visit: women full of advice on how to care for the ill, each fussing over favorite prescriptions, a great shifting and shuffling of their shawls.

"Eziquel cured my sister-in-law's uncle," Catarina's mother said.

"He's a very good man."

"The doctors in Sololá are for the dying."

"The *hospital* is for dying."

"Manuela, I know just what you need for swelling. Boil pine needles, *raiján,* loofah, thorns, alder, elderberry, *quina,* evergreen oak, the heart of pine, two eucalyptus leaves, mint leaves, lemon tea, and a box of Vicks. Bathe yourself with the mixture for half an hour."

One woman nodded throughout the recipe, then added her own: "Place crushed garlic and parsley in a bottle of honey. Let it sit for three weeks. Then drink a spoonful every hour for twenty days. It stops the aches in joints."

Isabel listened to the women take turns offering medications for her mother's various symptoms. Throughout it all, she imagined Allan Waters frantically drawing his pictures as names of plants *she* didn't even recognize swirled like a leaf storm around him.

"For fever, drink three cups of boiling hot mint tea and sit in the sweatbath for one hour."

"For fatigue, cut some branches off whatever plant you come across that is near a cross. When you get to the cross, use the branches to beat your legs. Toss the branches before the cross. Do this every day until the fatigue disappears."

They continued until each one of them had given her some recipe for swelling, fever, difficulty in breathing, and all the other things Manuela had complained about.

Her mother thanked them profusely. Isabel held the door open as they filed out of the house.

Her mother spoke very little to Isabel from the time the women left the house to the time her father returned from the field. She tried to help Isabel prepare food, but she tired fast and returned to bed. Isabel spoke once or twice, but her mother kept an irritated silence. It was punishment for speaking with the American and for bringing down the disapproval of the neighbors.

After Alfredo entered, the family ate sitting beside Manuela. She remained silent throughout dinner. Alfredo, thinking it was her illness, stroked his wife's leg through the thick blanket. The children finished quickly, and Isabel turned to the cleaning. The boys helped get Marcelina into bed, then went to their own mats. Isabel wiped the dishes and tried to hear her mother as she spoke in a hushed voice to her father.

Alfredo stepped from behind the partition with dishes in hand. "What did the American want?"

He asked with disarming calmness, she thought. "He's here to study medical things. He says he wants to help." She tried to speak calmly, too, not wanting her nervousness to provoke her father's anger as it had her mother's.

He sighed and sat wearily by the door, eyes leveled out into the night. "It's dangerous, Isabel."

"He seems honest, Father." And then by way of showing how safe it was, "He's not yet a man."

79

Her father grimaced. "It's dangerous."

"But what if he can help? What if he knows something?"

"What if he brings trouble?"

She placed the dishes in a pile on the low table and stared at her hands.

"Anything new," her father explained patiently, "is very dangerous, Isabel. People are afraid. You're still so young. You don't know. Something that can seem innocent can hold a terrible poison. That's the way it is here. The poor have no possibility of changing anything—"

"I don't want to believe that!"

Alfredo looked back in surprise. She spoke in the small alcove between herself and the wall, but her voice carried not one shred of the shyness her body showed. He got up and stood beside her.

"You want to help your mother."

Isabel struggled not to cry.

"You want to go to school."

He took such a deep breath that Isabel looked up, half afraid that he too was struggling with something. But he smiled and held her hands.

"It's my fault," he confessed. "I thought I could have my children go to school. I thought they could do something just a little bit better. But I have nothing more to give, Isabel. I'm a woodcutter, not a store owner. Look at my feet." He stepped back. "Look at your clothes."

She could look at neither.

"We are the poorest in a poor village. The center of the world is somewhere very far away. It will never be near us."

Isabel lost her struggle against crying. Alfredo held her tightly.

"I'm sorry," he said. "It was my stupid idea." He rocked her as she cried. And then his voice came close, so close that it nestled beside her ear and became something only she could hear: "You were the one," he whispered. "You were the one I hoped the most for."

The words shocked her; they knocked the wind out of her crying. It was a strange and wonderful confession. She could not understand it all as she stood enfolded in his loving embrace. What had he expected of her? What plans did he have for her? Did he want her to teach, too? Suddenly another blow came to her ears, and it took her father's lunge toward the door to make her realize it was something outside smashing against their house, not her emotions making her rock. José scrambled to the door before she could move.

Outside, by the gate, Alfredo peered through the darkness to listen for sounds. The night fog masked everything. By his feet, a red candle burned inside a circle of pine branches. Next to the candle lay a tuft of hair tied with a woman's ribbon. Isabel smelled burned hair. She squatted beside José. He pointed out the scorched ends and reached to grab the tuft.

"Leave it!" Alfredo shouted, nailing José's hand in mid-reach.

"What is it?"

But their father pulled on his cloak of privacy.

"What does it mean?" Isabel asked.

He spoke from deep inside that cloak. "I don't know."

José drew his arm back to his side. "What could it

mean?'' He asked no one, really; he spoke to the strange circle itself.

"Trouble,'' Alfredo whispered, so softly that his children barely heard.

"But why?'' Isabel protested.

That was all Alfredo would say. His privacy created such an implacable wall that Isabel and José moved toward the house. Their father remained by the gate as Isabel turned to glance back. And he remained as José, looking down, found the stone that had been cast against their home. Alfredo remained outside even as Isabel and José fell asleep, waiting and waiting for him to come inside.

Eight

Her mother seemed only to get worse. Aches lingered in the machinery of her joints, flutters in her heart were as common as spiders, and the swellings that before came and went like the ebb and flow of the lake water now settled and deepened like virulent tide pools. Alfredo had decided that none of them should tell Manuela about the terrible sign left at their gate. It could only make her worse, he had proclaimed to his children. If she knew that there were people wishing to do them harm—for whatever reason! he had said when Isabel began to protest—she would surely have more collapses. As a result, all of them moved in and out of the house, around one another, particularly around Manuela, with a gray sobriety and a grayer secretiveness.

Isabel watched her father come in from cutting wood to sell, or from the fields where he weeded, or from his attempts at bringing home fish. He seemed to grow older every day. His drink at night produced not the usual lessons or stories, but an intense and forlorn staring out into the distance. He would not hear what his children said to him and only spoke to give some quick and quiet order. Even as he helped Manuela in her rituals and to take the medicine Eziquel had prescribed, he wore his cloak of privacy so tightly around his shoulders that he seemed like one in mourning. Only sometimes would Manuela's spirits lift enough to make the family think that now, finally, this thing had passed. But these moments would be brief, and instead of giving hope, they would increase the empty expression on Alfredo Pacay's face.

"I'm going to die," Manuela said.

Alfredo reprimanded her: "Do not even say it!"

Once, Isabel said, "We should go to Sololá."

Her father turned angrily, fearfully. "The hospital is where people die!"

Yet another time, Alfredo came in later than usual with a bottle of Venado already in hand, the others having eaten and Marcelina asleep on her mat. He sat against the doorjamb, looking out into the fog that had descended on the village. It was white, solid, and impenetrable just a few feet from the door. He stared into the white bank as if in the cool emptiness there might be something yet to be read, some swirl of color or shadowed break that would allow the farther mountains or the lake or the lights from distant villages to magically appear and give a reassurance of the order of things. But the bank of fog stood solid and immoveable before him, a reflection of himself.

"Maybe I should sell animals," he said from out of his reverie.

Isabel looked around her. José sat in his underwear, tying the broken straps of his rubber sandals. Diego turned his top by hand in a lazy, sleepy fashion. She sat by the dead fire sewing patches of cloth she had found by the lake into José's worn pants. Beside her was the basket of corn Marcelina had abandoned in favor of sleep.

"I can buy a steer in Santiago," he mused aloud.

Isabel looked again to see to whom he was speaking. She was the only one who was still active in the business of the home.

She ventured softly: "Where will you get the money?"

Her father did not turn, nor did he react as if the voice he heard were anything but his own mind challenging this new idea. "Borrow it." He pensively sipped his rum, instead of downing the whole bottle. "I can get the foreign companies to turn the land into coffee."

"That takes money," she countered.

His tongue flicked out against a sliver of lime.

"They'll give me money to start."

"But that's for starting."

"I won't use it all for coffee. I'll buy an animal, too."

"And if it dies?"

"Hm."

"And the land won't be yours anymore."

Alfredo turned to Isabel. "We need to do something."

The word *we* socked into Isabel with as much force

85

as his earlier hint of some plan for her. She felt proud that he spoke to her not as a child, but as an equal, as he would to her mother late at night when the children dozed and the business of the home needed some discussion. He was getting her help, her advice. He spoke as easily and as naturally to her as he would to Manuela. But coiling around the pride over this confidence were the unwanted implications, as well. He was, by that naturalness, assuming what she had been secretly dreading for so many days. She was becoming the mother of the house. Alfredo did not speak to José, the first son, but to her. A terrible finality was carried within that *we*.

Isabel recalled little sacrifices she had witnessed in her own mother: Manuela taking a piece of chicken from her plate and placing it on Diego's plate; Manuela keeping silent when Marcelina in a childish tantrum said that she hated her mother; Manuela, with a small smile, drawing a comforting hand across the frightened face of her oldest daughter. The pettiness of the incidents surprised Isabel. She wondered why her mind would recall these things and not more important sacrifices, more serious times, like . . . and she could not recall a single one. Then she understood that it was the insignificant events that spoke more strongly of what parenthood meant. Like leaving school, to some. These small sacrifices told her that motherhood was not a grand landscape dotted with large and poignant markers, but was mostly a simple, everyday road with no real beginning and no end in sight. It was a path without detours, without places to rest. And though there were sister travelers, no one praised those who made the difficult and isolated journey. It was assumed to be the only journey a woman could take. Because of that, praise wasn't given for taking it; alarm was raised for *not* taking it.

Isabel wanted to answer her father, who still looked at her for a response. She wanted to give him an answer that would solve the dilemma, return them to normalcy, include them both, while not giving up any shred of hope for herself. She looked at him and felt sudden fear welling inside her. She did not know what the answer would be. What she knew was that she was not smart enough or old enough to give such a simple *and* complex answer. She could not help herself, so how would she be able to help him? She was too young! Still a child! Her father should be telling her, not the other way around.

With this tumult of fear and doubt cresting inside her, she saw in her father's sad face that he really did not want a solution. He sought merely a sound, a gesture, something that would ease the knot of sadness inside his chest. She suddenly recalled an episode when she was a little girl: Her mother stood behind her father and massaged his shoulders. She did not know it then, but now she understood that he had been crying. Not hard, like a baby, but softly, terribly softly and hidden, half ashamed, the way a man cries. Her mother had her face turned straight up to the ceiling as she rubbed, as if to keep the cup of her eyes balanced level and upward so that her own tears would not fall and scald her husband's defenseless skin. She knew that what her father wanted now was for her to quietly give him back his strength, to give him back power in a world that had always stolen it from him.

Isabel faced down to her sewing, away from his pleading eyes, and jabbed her needle into the cloth. "Father," she said, and pulled the needle through and up into the air, strongly, confidently, "you will find the best way." Her stomach churned with an uncertainty she dared not show. All of this was too new for her.

Her father dropped his gaze.

"If there's a way," she said more loudly, more easily, "Father, you will find it. As you always have."

The next day, while her mother slept and all was quiet except in her mind, which echoed with her father's thunderous *we,* Isabel went up the path toward the ruins of Oro Hill. She walked up the narrowest footpaths between rows of corn and fruit cacti to avoid Lucas and the other men laying the waterline. She walked among the coffee trees, up the hills, between lines of beans. She reached out for *buenaleña* branches to pull herself up sharp inclines. She avoided the machetes and hoes speaking in the fields. She turned from the deep *thunk* of axes calling from the trees and passed quickly, surreptitiously, over plateaus. She walked until the sloping field she ascended had only Juan Catú's steer, grazing meagerly around the rocks. The sky was a hot blue.

She turned a slow circle to see the horizons. The wall of mountains was dark green, the bowl of the lake a patchwork of colors. Closer, the rocks were in elaborate jumbles: stacked high or tumbled, built in precarious towers or huddling to make complex niches. Imbedded in some were pitaya cactus; in others, unripe prickly pears. On one side, a huge *hormigo* tree hunched down;

on the other side, jacaranda blossoms spilled into the desert-hot afternoon. It seemed, here, within the vastness of the lake, the dots of hamlets below, and in the solitude, that her problems would be overshadowed. A hummingbird appeared close by. The wings grunted as it zipped to the blossoms. It would not hold still. It flew off and returned, but so quickly and with such fear of her that she backed slowly into the rocks to keep the nervous bird in sight.

She waited in the rocks, hidden from sight, and peered out from a cranny. The small cave was so comfortable, so secure and cool, that she forgot about the hummingbird and found herself leaning back to look out through her small window at the same view she had earlier taken in with openness. The framing by the rocks gave her an odd sense of security, as if she could hold all of it and keep it. Her world seemed manageable, from the cool shelter of the rocks. The small grunting came again. She watched sympathetically the frightened *tzunún*. The hummingbird hovered and darted until it was sure no one saw, then sat for a moment on a branch some ten feet away. Its tiny head cocked repeatedly, its eyes peered fearfully all around, and then it flew off.

A stone clattered from above. She heard pebbles grinding underfoot, and suddenly a boot crunched inches from her face. The black boot twisted and lifted out of sight. Instantly, the man's whole body appeared on the slope. She heard hushed voices in Spanish. The man turned. He wore jungle fatigues, a floppy hat that shadowed his brow, and had a rifle in hand. On his face were black camouflaging streaks. He called to the other voices. There were more steps, the minute clattering of stones, and other men appeared. All had machetes strapped high on their backs. One man had rope and a backpack, one carried a radio, and one held a mortar launcher. All had ammunition belts. The first man Isabel had seen now stood pointing at Catú's grazing steer.

Isabel had seen all the weaponry before, when the military entered the village, but these men seemed different. They wore no badges or insignia. The uniforms were dirtier. She pushed herself deeper into the niche, drawing her knees up tight to hide herself as best she could. When she felt the sun on her brow, she pulled her face further back into shadow. She watched.

The men quickly sliced through the rope that tied the animal to a nearby tree. She knew what they would do. The dumb beast lumbered behind them to the slight plateau in front of the rocks. Several men worked to bind the front and back legs. Tied, the steer fell on its side like a lifeless tree. Its thick tongue licked stupidly from its mouth. One man knelt quickly by the head, temporarily blocking Isabel's view. When he stood again, he came up pulling a rope to force the animal's head straight back against its spine. The lower horn scratched a rut into the ground. Another man, with a long bayonet, appeared in front. He pressed along the animal's chest, touching the bones, feeling along the taut muscles; then he placed the point of the knife against the flesh. Using the heel of his hand and the brace of his own chest, he plunged the blade deep. Instantly, blood leaped from the wound. The man lurched backward in his scramble to get out of the way; the steer jerked and struggled as its blood spurted more than a meter. Blood and white liquid foamed from the animal's nostrils in its desperate fight for air. With each heave of its lungs, a fountain of blood arched up and out. Isabel's own breathing became labored as she watched the animal gasp. One man kept touching the steer's eye, causing the eyelid to flicker, the animal to lurch harder.

It took several minutes for the steer to grow too weary to constantly struggle. It heaved less violently, the arc of blood became smaller, the eyelid moved less under the probing finger. Instead, the lurches came after short lulls, as if the animal were gathering strength or as if the muscles were working free of life. Finally, the steer seemed to falter. The men still held the ropes, expecting the animal to gather itself for one final and violent struggle for life. When it came, the man holding the head rope was knocked to one knee. At last, the eyes felt nothing of the intrusive fingers. One of the men pressed his foot into the steer's belly and set up his own rhythm against the diaphragm. Blood spurted anew. Already the vast puddle by the dead animal was a soup of flies.

When no more blood came, the men let the ropes slacken. They did not speak, but sat among the rocks to smoke cigarettes. Isabel had no doubt that if they found her, these men—military or guerrillas—would kill her with the same coolness they had shown in killing the steer. Her breathing was now a small balloon kept close to her chin.

Minutes later, the men began butchering. They opened the belly and sliced out the purplish bladder of guts and entrails. They cut the forelimbs, around the skull, down the legs, and peeled back the skin with barely a concern for damaging the hide. They worked silently and quickly, dressing out the carcass with far less care than in butchering she had seen for market.

This meant that they were hurrying so as not to be seen. This meant that time was on her side in the deadly gamble of not being discovered.

The men moved awkwardly around the carcass. From their gruesome huddle there leaped out forelocks, the tail, liver, stomachs, blood-spattered parts that would be left for waste. They were taking only what could be dried, what would not spoil quickly, what was most efficient. The squandered pieces were cast off like sloppy leaves from a tree. They fell in different directions, landing on rocks, draping over low branches, settling in dirt, piling together. Isabel could smell intestine and blood. Their red scattering brought more flies, more insects, so that above the pool of blood a black swirling of wings grew larger by the minute. The men sawed and hacked, cracked joints, and ripped apart tendons, all the while flaying the air to drive away the flies. They waved their machetes and bayonets and only succeeded in scattering blood and bits of flesh onto one another. The more they fanned the air, the more they covered themselves, and the more they attracted flies. Even the small space of Isabel's cave buzzed with flies. She jerked her head to keep her eyes on the men. One frustrated soldier leaped up with a flurry of arms and stomped directly toward Isabel. She sucked her breath in and pushed back hard against the wall, into the shadows. Flies walked across her mouth and chin. She dared not move.

But the man seemed too bothered to notice her. He smacked at his arms, flicked off strands of flesh from his uniform, and vigorously rubbed his face, now streaked with blood and bits of skin.

"Come on!" the others said.

The man slapped at his chest.

Isabel could not bear the flies climbing on her face, tickling the inside of her nose, and moving blithely across her lips. She jerked her head and blew a short burst of air from her mouth. The flies lifted off to buzz inches from her face. Behind the blue and black swirl, she saw the man peering into the rocks. He leaned on one knee and stared into the shadows in her direction. His body remained absolutely still, attentive; Isabel watched the flies move over his face.

Then he stepped forward. The others had stopped and waited for action. Only the drone of insects could be heard. The man took another step, his feet barely making a sound on the rocks. The others carefully lifted their guns and turned in different directions, the heap of butchered flesh at their center. The man stepped silently toward Isabel with his long knife poised in front. The blade was dull with blood, and a thin strand of flesh dangled from one side.

Just as Isabel thought he might have seen her, he really did look right at her. His eyes shifted and locked. Isabel's hands clamped over her mouth and neck to keep from screaming. But he did not move. He stared deep into her eyes. His face stayed emotionless. Then his tongue peeked from between his lips and flies rearranged themselves on his face. He stared into her. She saw him thinking, judging, and then he turned to the others.

"Nada," he said. Nothing.

The other men put their guns by their sides and resumed their work. The man who had seen her stepped over the steer and turned to face in her direction. She thought for an instant that he could still see her. He looked up once, checked the rocks around her, but then went back to his butchering.

He was a young Indian, but not a Tzutujil, at least not from this part of the lake. Isabel let the flies wander freely on her face. She dared not move until the soldiers finished and walked completely out of sight and hearing, and she did not move for a long time after, as well.

Nine

On Sunday, the center was crowded with church-goers, most of them more interested in the news that the waterline would be finished Tuesday than in the imminent mass. The celebration for the water excited everyone as they waited patiently for Father Ordoño to arrive from Santiago Atitlán.

As usual, there were far more women going to church than men. Without exception, the women dressed in traditional clothes, whereas men dressed in traditional pants and belts yet with ladino shirts, hats, and shoes. What linked the men and women, perhaps, was that both the women's scarves and the men's belts were a blue-green iridescence, like the sparkling hummingbird.

Outside the small stone church, the women stood together, their finest shawls folded in half lengthwise and placed over one shoulder. The men sat under trees,

leaned against walls, or stood proudly in full view—
thumbs hooked into belts, hats cocked slightly forward,
a sockless shoe planted flat on the wall behind. Those
who could afford shoes shined them; those who had sandals or no shoes at all were scorned. The men wore
their best knee-length pants and finest sash belts. Atop
their heads were wheat-colored cowboy hats, some with
small feathers, some with more flamboyant taffeta
scarves tied around so that the ends trailed like rooster
tails. All but the oldest men wore their shirts unbut-
toned to the middle of their chests.

Males tended to stand apart from the females, and
the females remained close to the small church door.
The men held back until it was time to enter.

Isabel's family had walked slowly up the hill, Manuela barely making three meters in a minute. Everyone
wished her well, though there was a great whispering
like an effusion of gnats once they passed. Manuela did
not notice, but Isabel did and thought of the lock of
hair by the gate. José and Diego ran ahead to join
friends, so that Isabel was left alone with her mother
and Marcelina. Alfredo had gone out on the boat to fish
and see if God wouldn't do him a little favor if the rest
of the family went to church.

"Every year they get smaller," he had said of the
fish. "Every year the water darker. You go. Perhaps
something will come of your prayer."

So they had gone, slowly, up the hill, the four of
them. Near the center, the boys hurried off like rabbits
at a ball game. Isabel saw her girl friends by the church
door. Lucas stood nearby with two other young men.
He looked at her for an instant, too fast for her to wave

hello. Not far from him, Teresa smiled and waved. She had new shoes. Isabel looked down at her bare and calloused feet as she and her mother continued slowly toward the church. They paused at the entrance, her mother breathing hard enough to warrant a rest. She put a hand on the cool stone.

Inside, two of the four men who played for the church warmed up by playing snatches of folk songs. Several other men swept the floor and arranged the pews. Three women brought a table to the doorway and greeted Manuela with warm smiles. They set up a box and two silver chalices, one with the host, the other with a pair of tongs. Isabel and Manuela each placed ten centavos into the box, then used the tongs to pinch out a host. Isabel helped her mother kneel at the door before entering. They covered their heads with their shawls. Isabel had to pull her mother up by the shoulders, and then they limped to the front left rows.

It was customary for the men to wait outside until the women filled the front rows. Later, when word came that Father Ordoño had really arrived, they would sit in the farthest rows, even if there were empty pews between the women and men. Father Ordoño would enter the small room to the side of the church and hold quick confessions before mass. Except for those with the altar boys, these confessions were all with women.

The mass was expected to begin soon, give or take an hour. Sometimes the father didn't arrive, and everyone would sit in the church and outside for hours, the rhythms of the musicians crescendoing, then stopping anticlimactically in waves that emulated the increasingly broken expectation of mass.

97

It was a simple church. The altar was a wood table; the alcove had no statuary, but a large mural depicting a very young and very white Jesus with arms outstretched in such a way as to encompass all of the lake below him. Under one arm, a man worked his field, under the other, a woman carried an urn on her head. Both Indians were dressed in full traditional clothes. Growing up from the ground at Jesus' feet, a single stalk of corn curved and wove its leaves under His nurturing gaze.

They waited patiently. All the musicians arrived and they continued their tinkering. A woman by the aisle pulled the pants down on her whining child. The little boy urinated under the pew. More people entered the church. The front rows filled, and a few men sat in the last pew.

When at last Father Ordoño arrived, he arrived with a surprise. An American stepped out of the father's red Ford Bronco. He told those nearby that the stranger was a priest from a place called Oklahoma. As a special treat, the newcomer would give mass. Within seconds, everyone in and out of the church knew that the bearded American with cowboy hat and boots would be performing the service. The two fathers entered the side room to change. The musicians now started to complete their songs instead of cutting them short. All who planned to attend mass, and some who hadn't until the American arrived, entered the church and filled the pews.

"Will he give confession?" Isabel whispered to her mother.

"Father Ordoño?"

"No, the other." She did not know if she would dare confess to the American.

"Will you go?"

Her mother asked the question bent into the pew, her body seemingly collapsing into the hard angles of the seat. Her mother was ill, worsening, needing attention, and yet Isabel's own mind searched for wings. She recalled Lucas's face when he had challenged her about what she really wanted.

"Yes, I will," she answered.

Perhaps it was better that it was an American. Allan Waters had somehow become a part of this. He had worked his way, unwittingly, into the whole situation. She rose. "Are you all right?"

"Go," Manuela said into her lap.

"Okay."

Isabel walked down the aisle, past Teresa and Lucas Choy; past Rosario, Helisabet, and Catarina; past Josefa, Rosa, María, and Catarina's mother; past all those waiting and watching in the pews. The chords of the mandolin alone followed behind her.

In the other room, only a board separated her from Father Ordoño. Despite her thoughts just moments before, she was glad it was not the American.

"My mother is ill. She cannot even lift things. She can't breathe at night. Her feet get as fat as her legs. She can't do anything."

"Pobrecita."

"She tries to lift the pots from the fire and she can't do it. When she goes to bring in wood, it's as if she were bringing in a tree."

The father said nothing.

99

"She gets tired so fast. All she can do is lie in bed. She suffers so much."

"What is bothering you, my child?"

"I get angry that I have to do all the work."

She could almost hear him smile. "That is normal," he said. "That's not a sin."

"But I think only of myself, not about my duties to the family."

"Do you do anything wrong?"

"Oh, no, Father."

"Do you have sinful thoughts?"

"I feel confused. I don't know what to do."

"Do you think of hurting your mother?"

"If I go away to school to teach—"

"No, no. Do you want to hurt her? Is she taking so much time that you want to hurt her?"

"No."

"Do you have evil thoughts about your brothers or your father?"

"No."

"Are you engaged in witchcraft or the practice of idolatry?"

"No."

"Do you have lust in your heart?"

"No!"

"My child, you are young and bothered by normal concerns. Pray, and let God's guidance enter you. Listen to Him with your heart. Believe in Him who has made you, and He will surely help you. There is no sin in you, my child, only the confusions of life. God helps us if we open ourselves to Him."

"But I feel so bad."

"Now, now. You're not a sinner. Pray."

"Pray?"

"Yes." He cleared his throat. "Now let the next person in."

"Thank you, Father."

"Pray, my child. Pray every day."

One older woman waited outside. She gazed up as Isabel passed, but Isabel looked away. She did not want to face anyone. To her surprise, Allan Waters stood at the door of the church with a tape recorder and clipboard. He stopped her as she went to pass him.

"Please," he said reaching a hand out.

Isabel froze before he touched her. All she could think about was the bundled hair and the wreath of pine branches.

"I understand your mother is ill."

"Yes."

He shifted on his feet. "Can I speak with her?"

"No."

"How about with you?"

"No." She saw several people looking back at them, her mother among them.

"I just want to talk about symptoms. Just about the illness."

More faces turned, though they certainly could not hear.

"I think maybe I can help. And you can help me, of course."

Teresa stared back, too, an odd expression on her face.

"Perhaps by speaking about the symptoms she can

get help from a doctor and I can see what might work with my ideas. It wouldn't take long at all.''

Suddenly Lucas's face became more visible than the others. His eyes narrowed; his face had a darkness she had never seen in him. He seemed to be judging her; some idea began coalescing into something hard and real. When he turned slowly away, it was as if the motion took away all the warmth from her body. She clutched her shawl and walked quickly past Allan—''Wait!'' he cried in vain—and she hurried to the seat beside her mother without the minutest turn of her head. She kept her eyes straight ahead, even when her mother made a noise in her throat, even when the musicians signaled with ''When the Saints Go Marching In'' that Father Ordoño and the American priest were walking up the aisle.

Father Ordoño sat to the side of the long altar. The American knelt and crossed himself. He went through the ritual of sanctifying and blessing. And when he finished blessing the altar and cleansing his hands, he removed a handkerchief and thunderously blew his noise.

The musicians had just begun to play ''Amazing Grace.''

Ten

The following Tuesday, the village forgot all its troubles. The long scar of the waterline seemed an old wound finally healed through the hard efforts of the people of Chuuí Chopaló. The copper faucet gleamed like polished bronze in the center. Eventually there would be a large public basin, a *pila,* so the women could wash clothes and the soap could filter through the ground before entering the lake. For now, it would be a place to get clean water pumped from out deeper than the shoreline. The pump, brought by the mayor and two other men from Guatemala City, stood like an odd assortment of metal under a slanting cornstalk roof, and looked like a pile of junk that would never be transformed into something useful.

In the Pacay household, José talked excitedly about Los Tzutujiles, a band from Santiago Atitlán, which would play before the soccer game. He talked excitedly to the family about the mayor, who would speak at the turning on of the water just before the game. He talked about how everyone would be at the soccer field. In short, he spoke excitedly about everything connected to the celebration so that he could tag on the subject of the soccer game—a game he was more than a little proud to be in.

That morning, Isabel watched her father lead her brothers and sister out of the house. They did not look back once at her in the doorway. All around, the sounds of laughter swept them away into the frothy excitement carrying everyone up to the center. No one noticed Isabel staring forlornly after them. And it seemed to her more than ever that laughter could be a bitter thing when one was outside of it.

Behind her, Manuela asked to have a glass of water and for Isabel to prepare the medicine. Isabel tore herself away from the doorway and did as she was told. She longed to see the mayor dressed in his suit and tie like someone from the capital. She imagined him speaking eloquently about how Chuuí Chopaló would not be like other villages now that it had water and a central *pila,* but now it really would soar above the Lake–sea. She imagined the pump starting with a roar like that of the buses that ran to and from Santiago. She imagined it coughing out a long plume of black smoke and then chugging as it labored to pull the water uphill.

Her mother lay in bed with her arms flat by her side and her face tensed in pain when Isabel brought her the water. It seemed that she was trying to relax into the pain, as if to tame it by mentally dominating it or by flying above it through sheer force of will. She did not want to break her mother's concentration.

But her mother spoke. "Put it down."

Her voice was full of strain, as if her words were hard little things she had to force through the narrow aperture of her throat.

Isabel returned to adjust a pot of water on the fire, then snapped two small branches of myrtle. She looked back to see if her mother was watching to make sure she made the medicine correctly, but Manuela still lay in her private battle. As Eziquel had instructed, Isabel lit the branches by placing the ends in the fire. She poured two cups of boiling water. In these, she extinguished the branches and stirred the floating ash and wood bits to make tea.

"Do you want them now?" she asked, barely above a whisper.

Her mother nodded.

Isabel sat beside her. Neither moved for several moments. The squirrel in the roof scratched, then leaped to a nearby tree. They were in a cocoon of silence. Their world was a swaddled and protected cove, the outside so distant that none of its tendrils of sound crept through the breaches in the walls to molest them. In this cocoon, Isabel began to believe her mother could win against any illness. Fortified against the unfortunate things of the world around them, she would have a place to combat the demons torturing her body and soul.

Isabel put her head back against the wall and closed her eyes. In her mind, she formed the idea of her mother's illness into a faceless monster with swollen limbs and blue veins. It crawled in her imagination like some ugly lizard sneaking through brush or crawling under moss-covered stones.

When she opened her eyes to erase the horrible thing from her brain, she saw her mother staring up at her.

"Are you all right?" she asked.

Isabel shrugged involuntarily. "Yes, Mami."

Her mother looked at her the way someone who has just awakened looks at her surroundings: trying to focus and seeing everything as too bright, too new. Her hand went up to her face and rubbed across her forehead.

Isabel bent forward to pass the medicine. The cups were hot; steam licked up from the light green water. Manuela smiled feebly and took hold of the first cup. She blew cooling breath into it and sipped. She seemed like an old, old woman to Isabel, and for an instant Isabel tried to see herself as old and wrinkled, as in the last years of her own life. She felt her mother's free hand squeeze her own.

"I know this is hard for you."

Isabel looked at the ground between them.

"I know," Manuela said again.

With those simple words, something unnameable lifted away from Isabel. She felt a sudden release coming from her stomach, then something warm and relaxed washing in to take the place of what had left. Without a specific thought in her head, just the change coming on like the turn of a spigot or the flick of a match, she cried. Not hard, but softly, untying the knot that had been bundling up tight inside her chest without her knowing it.

Her mother pulled her hand with such gentleness that

it was like a secret whisper that drew her forward and down to lie beside her mother. There, Isabel felt like a little girl again, protected within her mother's embrace. But her own strength of body was too sharp a contrast to the frailty of her mother, so that Isabel quickly recoiled, both afraid that she would crush her mother's bones and suddenly ashamed that she could act like such a whimpering child when her mother was gravely ill. Isabel dabbed her face with the sleeves of her blouse and stood up.

"Go," Manuela said softly.

Isabel straightened her back. "What?" She wiped the streaks off her face.

Her mother sipped from the cup, sucking in air to cool her mouth. She drank without answering until half was gone.

"I'm tired," she said. "As soon as I finish, I'm going to sleep."

Isabel looked at the door, still uncertain as to what her mother meant.

"You need to enjoy yourself."

The fire smoldered a few feet away. There were no sounds outside the hut. Everyone would be in the center.

"But—"

"Go see," she said, her face like a mask. She held the cup with both hands, rolling the warm sides in her palms before drinking.

Isabel awkwardly brushed at her skirt, checked her blouse. She'd have to wash her face and hands. Comb her hair. She should put a ribbon in her hair like the one she had tied into Marcelina's braids.

107

"You look beautiful," her mother said.

Isabel blushed.

"You've always been beautiful."

Isabel looked up and saw a real happiness in her mother's eyes.

"My beautiful daughter," Manuela breathed. "Go."

Everyone had moved from the spectacle of the waterline to the soccer field further up the road. Isabel approached and heard music and shouting long before she rounded the bend to see the field. With each step she took, she felt lighter and happier, as if the music were filling her lungs and arms to create within her a special buoyancy. Past the center, she started to run. A flock of brown birds followed briefly and noisily until they turned into the trees. Isabel's heart pounded with excitement.

It seemed that the entire village surrounded the playing field. A small congregation—Teresa within it—sat by the simple stage where the band played; another milled by some of the soccer players, but the majority spread out and sat on the dirt banks of the soccer field periphery. Isabel slowed down and approached cautiously, not wanting to draw attention to herself. She knew she could not stay long, and she didn't want anything to steal her enjoyment—no strange looks at her, or odd comments, or awkward exchanges. She wanted only to locate her family and stand with them to watch her brother play.

She felt a bittersweet thrill when she saw that Lucas was also playing. He was among the oldest boys, and among the best, and despite their difficulties, she could not help but watch him deftly take the ball past several boys and up the field. His shorts and T-shirts showed off his muscular body. She watched him so intently that she failed to see Marcelina skip up and try to scare her with a shove at the back of her knees. Isabel nearly collapsed as her knees buckled.

Marcelina became all laughter and motion as she scampered away toward the others. Isabel set up the chase, to Marcelina's delight.

"I'll get you!" Isabel yelled, eliciting a squeal from her young sister.

They scuttled across the field, Isabel pretending to struggle, Marcelina almost, nearly, just about hoping she would not be caught. Finally, Isabel scooped up Marcelina in mid-stride and lifted her high in her arms, a bundle of happy flesh in a tousled skirt. Victorious, Isabel hefted her laughing sister onto her shoulder like a bag of grain and paraded across to where her father and Diego stood.

Alfredo could not keep his worry from showing when he asked about his wife.

"She told me to come," Isabel explained, letting Marcelina slide down to the ground. "She's fine. She said she was fine." Marcelina did not want to be put down. "Stop! Really, Father, she said I could— Ouch! You pest!" She gathered Marcelina back up into her arms. "All right, but only if you don't squirm."

Alfredo glanced down the path. "I'll go see how she's doing."

"No!" Isabel became instantly embarrassed at the strength of her voice. She felt her happiness disappear with her father's concern. "I'll go back, Father." She looked at Marcelina and smiled bravely.

Marcelina whined, "No."

Alfredo realized he had inadvertently taken away Isabel's chance to just enjoy the day and not think about her mother's illness. "I'm sorry," he said. "You're right. Of course she's fine. No one needs to go back right now. We'll stay for a while."

Marcelina's innocent and exuberant "Yes!" spoke for them all, but particularly for Isabel.

"Till halftime," he added.

Diego was oblivious to it all and stared excitedly at the boys passing the ball or attempting to carry it past an insurmountable number of opponents. A boy the same age as Diego ran onto the field and tried to steal the ball, but the older boys shouted him off. This warm-up was as important as the game—perhaps more important—because the boys could pretend great skill with no risk and yet have the opportunity to look wonderful in front of their peers and the girls they wished to awe.

"There's José," Marcelina shouted, pointing him out.

José stood way upfield with another group that passed the ball around. The family watched him stop a pass with his chest, flip the ball up with the point of his toe, and volley it for several seconds with his knees.

Marcelina clapped proudly for her brother.

"He's good," Isabel agreed, at the same time catching sight of Lucas as he used his head to lob a ball high into the air.

Marcelina jiggled shyly against her sister. "José is the best!"

Isabel, however, had her eyes on Lucas as he word-lessly formed a few of the boys into a circle to pass the ball with only their heads. He showed off by knocking it up five or six times before passing. None of the others could do it, and Isabel felt a warm pride seep into her limbs.

"Look at Lucas!" Marcelina said.

Isabel acted innocent. "Where?"

"There."

Alfredo smiled knowingly.

All of them watched the boys show off as they warmed up. The gaiety of the music and the energy of the cel-ebration seemed to obliterate any hard feelings that had wormed their way into people's hearts. Graciously, the sky was bright and few clouds passed overhead on this day when the village had something more precious than anything it had ever had before: water under its con-trol. Though barely more than a simple faucet, it sym-bolized for the farming community a dependable flow of water. Even more importantly, it was water coming to Above the Lake–Sea by virtue of their own work. It didn't matter that few of them could explain the exact nature of the symbol. Because it was water they were dealing with, and because they had pumped it up from the lake by their own works, it spoke loudly and clearly to their most basic need. The general happiness seemed infectious, so that everyone, even the band and neigh-bors from other hamlets, filled to overflowing with ex-citement. Allan Waters appeared on the periphery and joined the celebration.

The game began despite the players' desires to keep showing off in this safe way. The audience shouted encouragement and the boys gave friendly, competitive jeers and soon the names of the players rang out from the audience like monkey chatter. Isabel kept her eye on Lucas, and sometimes on José, when the two of them happened to pass close to each other. It was obvious that Lucas was much better than the rest. He easily sped past the other team when there were only one or two players in his way—a rare thing as the game developed. Neither team scored by the middle of the second quarter, but no one minded. They played enthusiastically, sometimes in coordination to almost make goals, but mostly as individuals, each seeking to be a hero. The audience loved it.

Teresa suddenly appeared beside Isabel. Before they could speak, Lucas stole the ball and pushed through two players. Isabel and Teresa each jumped forward, shouting his name with such energy that they both suddenly stopped. They looked at each other for a moment, then burst into laughter. Someone tripped Lucas and sent him tumbling to the ground. A fair number of the players were too bad for the game to be anything but fun. There were no long lulls of inactivity as sides got into place and skillfully dribbled downfield to make their plays. Instead, it was a melee, a horde moving herky-jerky up and down the field with only occasional bursts forward by a single person who managed to finagle the ball free for a brief sprint in the sun.

To Marcelina's immense joy, José was one of those who sometimes broke free of the pack with the ball skipping ahead. In no time at all, he would be blocked and boys would fall, an embroilment of arms and legs. Then the mob of players would descend on the successful blocker to take him down. Over the first and second quarters, Marcelina developed a pout in sympathy for José.

With each passing minute, Isabel knew she would have to leave. But what bothered her more was the fact that in all the time she had been watching, Lucas had not once looked her way, even during the brief quarter break. How she longed for them to just talk, away from the noise of everyone else. She wished she could speak to Teresa as well, to find out what things Lucas could have heard to make him put up his walls, but the place and time made it impossible. Teresa seemed far more interested in the game than in anything else. In any case, she could not speak to Teresa with her father so close. Leaving was out of the question except to return to the house to care for Manuela.

Isabel watched the game with new restraint. She no longer felt the excitement as only some inexorable tugging at her muscles and blood, but as something clearly about to end as well. She felt both extremes as she watched the final minutes of the first half: the thrill of the celebration and the certainty of an end—not just because she had to leave, but because all of it had to end and everyone would return to the drudgery and pettiness of daily life. It was a return to the specter of her mother's illness, the specter of ill will brought to the surface in the pine circle and bound hair. It was a return to the mysterious problem between Lucas and herself. For the first time, she understood with more than just her intellect what Maestro Xiloj had tried to explain one day about polarity, about everything having both life and death. "Whatever is begun," he had said, "always carries an end." He had been talking about how choices always eliminate possibilities—at least those options that were not taken—but he meant, as well, she realized now, that there is no such thing as a beginning without that final winding down. Then, as now, the idea conveyed to Isabel only a weighty sadness that made everything seem futile, no matter that Andrés Xiloj spoke about it in positive terms. "And nothing can die unless it first has lived," he had said excitedly. She still did not understand that part of it—that odd kind of optimism.

She tried forcing her attention on Lucas to try and squeeze what remaining joy she could from the game before she would have to head back to the solitude of the house. Teresa, of course, had sensed no change in her. She, like the others, was cheering for the final minutes. Even Allan Waters seemed a part of the village in the unrestrained celebration. Isabel saw him laughing with a group of boys. That, too, would surely end.

The referee's clock worked like a bellows, fanning oxygen into everyone's flame of excitement. Each minute ticked away as if there were only one clock in everyone's mind, and the fired audience got hotter, brighter until it roared like a bonfire. Teresa hopped, arms waving, face flushed from shouting. Isabel's sister and brother howled for José. Their flames reignited Isabel's low embers, and she found herself shouting and madly hopping, too.

Still there was no score. The players got more frantic. They shouted insults at one another. Two boys began a shoving match on the sidelines; men boasted about their sons. Through it all, the ball was the great catalyst. Wherever the ball went, the players followed like demons. Their manic onslaught was both comical and dangerous. The audience laughed at the minor squabbles for a heroic last-minute shot, at the tumbles the players collapsed into; and they shuddered at the kicked shins and bad falls. One boy crumpled onto the field and did not get up, his hands pressed high between his legs, his face pinched to the heavens. The others dashed after the ball and the unlucky boy who thought he could get it to the goal.

Suddenly Lucas bolted out from the center of the mass and sprinted ahead. Most of the players were too confused to know someone had escaped. The rest, José among them, packed after Lucas, attempting to trip and tackle him. But those who tried tackles fell like sticks onto the dust. Halfway down the field, only José and two boys pounded the ground after him. The goalie and another player braced themselves with looks of certain defeat.

Teresa squealed like a child and grabbed Isabel's arm with both hands. They hopped and danced, their skirts flapping around their calves. Marcelina and Diego rooted for José, but José, running wildly, tripped and went sprawling. Only the other two boys had any opportunity of catching Lucas. The rest of the players came running, but they were impossibly far behind.

The goalie's dread grew into a wide and pale mask. His teammate shifted nervously. Lucas dribbled within an easy six meters, his arms drumming to get into position, his fists clenching, body tensing to kick with all his might.

And in that moment, everyone grew silent with expectation. Time, of course, turned slow. Lucas's right leg angled back, his left leg dug into the earth for balance, his face brightened with concentration. With a solid *whoof,* the ball shot forward like a slow and silent dream of cannon fire. The speed and noise suddenly returned like a shot as the goalie, trembling with fear, threw himself at the ball with all his soul—and snatched it from the air like round fruit from a tree.

The field exploded with laughter and shouting. Lucas stood flabbergasted in front of the awestruck goalie. Teresa and Isabel stared dumbly at each other. The other players swept noisily down by the goal.

"Throw the ball, throw the ball!" the goalie's team shouted.

Several of his players circled by the sidelines, waiting for the goalie to wake up from his dream of success and get the final seconds going. The goalie glanced down into his hands and then up at Lucas.

Lucas could not believe that he had missed. He stared up to the sky that seemed full of laughter at a miss that should never have happened in a million years. He spun slowly around to face the other end in defeat.

The goalie tossed the ball to the corner, where the teams battled for control. Out popped the ball, with a player dribbling up the side and shouting for Lucas to turn, to get the pass—to hurry!

"Lucas!" he screamed, passing high over everyone's heads and straight for the center where Lucas still stood, angled toward the opposite goal, caught in a stupor of disbelief. The ball zoomed too fast for any thought, too fast for reason or planning, and Lucas simply threw himself into the air and flipped backward, legs like a

116

pinwheel over his head, the topside of his toe catching leather, his whole body nothing but intuition. When he landed in a heap, a roar whooshed up around him.

Isabel ran like a madwoman, her body also moving involuntarily toward the person she loved, the only young man who could make her body react so completely on its own. She didn't care what others might think or what they should or should not see. She wanted him alive, unhurt, and when she saw him untangle himself to sit awkardly on the ground, her chest pounded with hot relief. In that relief, her excitement focused on his unbelievable goal. She reached him before he knew she was rushing toward him and enfolded his head and shoulders in her full embrace. She rocked him hard in her exuberance. He laughed giddily and pulled her down beside him. Their arms wrapped around each other; their lips pressed together with such abandonment that the world dissolved to nothing around them.

Then the shock of what they had done came crashing down. They looked up at the scowling women, snickering boys, and at a strange expression on Teresa's face.

Isabel dropped her head in shame. Her face burned so hotly that she dared not look up. Lucas rose silently beside her, his bewilderment growing into an iciness. Suddenly, Isabel felt her father's hand snake around her upper arm to lead her away from Lucas and all the harshly staring people, those faces making strong judgments.

Eleven

Eziquel Coxol placed his hand on top of Manuela's head so she wouldn't bump it and helped her bow low into the sweatbath. Manuela clutched at herself as she bent into the small stone room behind the Pacays' hut. She hobbled on her swollen feet so that she seemed to be in a perverse dance, her upper body jerking and shuddering, her lower body on the verge of crumpling, all of her wrapping into a convulsive ball to fit through the narrow opening of the *temescal*.

Isabel could not look at her mother for very long without having a long shard of unhappiness lodge itself in her chest. She concentrated, instead, on her father's set expression. She tried to picture the two of them holding each other by the doorway, and herself as a small child. Her mother curled back into his arms. They sat folded into each other for hours, laughing occasionally, watching her play close by, their faces holding something secret between them, something manifested in private strokings, in the gentle pressing of his lips into her neck, in the unhurried brush of their faces— things she was just now beginning to understand: the warmth and closeness of real love. But in the present, each day weakened Manuela so much that Isabel's memory could be about her father and some other person. That was what caused her the most unexpected grief. What seemed like the imminent death of her mother was made many times worse by her mother's metamorphosis from a strong, vibrant woman into a weak and unhappy stranger.

Eziquel emerged from the *temescal* with sweat beading like tiny gemstones on his forehead. "One hour," he said. He drew a forefinger across his brow, then snapped the moisture to the ground.

Alfredo shifted nervously on his feet; his mouth moved to speak, but then he decided to chew his thought between his front teeth. The *sanjorín* plopped wearily on a flat rock. He glanced at the opening of the sweatbath. Isabel sat at a respectful distance, and Alfredo paced in a slow, tight line.

Isabel saw Eziquel turn his face upward to the sky. He stared up as if looking for an answer in the heavens. The features of his face were like small hills perfectly set against a blue sky, each peak reaching up for something from Heart of Heaven, or the Christian God, or simply the forces of Wind and Sun. Then the peaks of his profile turned slowly toward her.

"She has taken the medicine every day as I instructed?"

"Yes, Don Eziquel."

His eyelids drooped lazily over his eyes. He had worked with Manuela for hours now. "She has done what she should in the world?"

"Yes, Don Eziquel."

His fingers intertwined. "And she has rested."

"Yes," she answered before realizing that it hadn't been a question, but a running down of possibilities.

Alfredo's pacing slowed with each of the *sanjorín's* questions until he stopped quietly beside Isabel, arms hanging limply at his sides.

Eziquel's face turned upward again.

They could hear children not far away: boys, no doubt, playing with marbles or tops. A blackbird cocked its head on the fence at the back of the yard. The chickens scratched incessantly at the ground, their heads snapping from side to side to inspect everything underfoot. Manuela coughed from inside the *temescal*.

Isabel remembered Allan Waters standing by the soccer field, cheering with others at the game, being a part of them all for that brief moment of celebration.

"Perhaps . . ." she muttered, feeling her words break through some membrane that had grown all around them. She hesitated. Eziquel's face turned slowly down again, but he did not look at her. Alfredo sat back on his haunches beside her and looked up into her face. "Perhaps," she started again, "we can go to Sololá."

Eziquel's eyelids closed and opened.

Alfredo waited for a word from him, expecting only complaint.

Eziquel sighed. "Perhaps," he conceded.

Isabel breathed again.

Alfredo smiled. His face brightened with hope. His lips again moved with the idea he had previously chewed, feeling in this small concession an opening through which his thoughts could run. "Eziquel." His body angled forward. "I haven't told you all that has happened here."

The old man peered with interest.

"We have had signs. At first we found a circle of pine branches with a red candle and blood—"

The *sanjorín's* face darkened.

"—and then, after church last Sunday, a dead snake with its tail in its mouth."

"Who did this?"

Alfredo shrugged. "And last night, after the game, we found a jar full of insects."

Eziquel questioned Isabel with his eyes.

"I don't know who it is," she answered.

"When did it begin?"

Alfredo thought for a moment, but Isabel knew it as the day Allan Waters first came to the house.

"Ten days ago," her father said. "Maybe two weeks."

Eziquel Coxol crossed his arms.

"What does it mean?"

The *sanjorín* touched his pouch of divining beans, caressing the smooth leather with his fingers. He seemed lost in a search through his mental catalog of cures, bewitchings, black magic, and white magic.

But Isabel felt something more urgent, more immediate, struggling to get out: "Allan Waters said he can help."

Instantly these words turned into venom in the air between her and the two men. Alfredo scowled at her. "What does he know of spells?"

Isabel was shocked at the misunderstanding. Her mind had linked Waters and her mother, and not Waters and the warnings. "No," she said, "I mean he said he can help Mother."

Eziquel glared at her. "You must choose what you believe! Both of you!"

Alfredo nodded humbly.

"This daughter of yours thinks she knows more than others. She complains all the time about her duties—what any girl should feel happy to do—and prefers to turn against her own people."

Chagrined, Alfredo looked sideways at Isabel.

"Why hasn't she married, Alfredo?"

"Wait a minute," Alfredo cautioned. The *sanjorín* was overstepping his bounds.

"What is she waiting for?"

"This has nothing to—" Alfredo began languidly.

"Or does she prefer to kiss boys in the soccer field?"

Alfredo lunged at Eziquel.

"Father!" she screamed.

Alfredo had the old man in his hands. He shook him by the throat.

Isabel pulled at his arms. "Don't! Please!"

"Bastard!" he swore. He shook Eziquel as if he were a child in spite of Isabel's grappling.

Out of the corner of her eye, Isabel saw José running toward them. She called for help.

José, however, came panting for another reason. He did not really notice the fighting between the men, he was so flustered. "The army's here!" he said. "They're in the center. They want everyone to come!"

Alfredo's hand dropped from the *sanjorín's* shirt.

Only then did José see what had been happening.

The children watched in amazement the battle of eyes between their father and Eziquel.

Alfredo spoke without turning from the old man, as if his words were directed at Coxol, too. "Go, José. Isabel too. See what stupid thing they have written. See how they have insulted us!"

The children did not budge at first, wanting to see how the conflict would be resolved. Because of sheer promised violence, Alfredo's glare humbled the old man out of the compound and down the road and away from their home.

"Go," Alfredo said to his children.

They hurried to the center. All around them, frightened older children and adults hurried as well. A thread spun out from their fear, and wove into and around each of them so that it loomed a frightening tapestry of Chuuí Chopaló in the foreground with the army as background of the cloth. Soldiers stood watching along the avenue on either side, Israeli rifles in both hands. The only protection for the villagers was their silence and obedience.

Two dozen more soldiers encircled the perimeter of the center, where many of the villagers already waited apprehensively. The officer stood by the stone cross, flanked by three others. These men held their rifle barrels out, parallel to the round at waist height. The officer was the only one with a pistol, the established sign of rank. He carried no other weapon. In his right hand was a paper he twisted into a cone. He began to tap the point of the cone rhythmically at his hip.

Isabel scanned the faces to find Lucas beside Teresa and other schoolmates. They remained partially hidden by elder men, who were required to be in the front. She dared not signal for fear of attracting the officer's attention and remained by José with an unattainable desire to step cautiously up to Lucas's side.

She watched the officer closely and waited with the others for what proclamation he deigned to give. She felt small and insignificant, her insides thrumming hard with emotion like a frantic hummingbird.

The officer spoke privately to one of the guards, who never took his attention from the congregating villagers and did not respond in any way to his superior.

A curious sense of familiarity struck Isabel. She looked carefully at one of the guards. It could be one of the men she had encountered butchering the steer, but she was not sure. Only one soldier had been sufficiently close for her to remember clearly. The others were logged in her mind more as emblems of danger than as individuals. They had all worn blacking on their faces. These men were clean. These uniforms were sharp, the shoes fairly new. And each had insignia on the rolled jungle fatigue sleeves. Their packs seemed shinier, their weapons more menacing. They could not be the same men, she decided. And what if they were? What would it mean? That the guerrillas were part of the military? That the army pretended to be a guerrilla team to sanction their fear tactics? Too many questions arose with those answers as well. Why wouldn't the army make more of a show when pretending to be guerrillas? Why would they use men who were bound to be recognized? How could the guerrillas trust men drawn from the military? And why did the movement seem more illusory than real? The guerrillas never even drew their symbols on the rocks like all the other political branches. Wouldn't they want to flaunt their power? They never spread propaganda that would give the poor villagers enough confidence to join their struggle. And what was the struggle about? Why didn't the guerrillas inundate the countryside with leaflets? It was too much of a puzzle for Isabel to figure out.

The only sure things were that the military generated fear every time they appeared; that many of the luxurious homes surrounding the lake were owned by the powerful and rich of Guatemala, including the president; and that confusion sired by contradictions reigned supreme. Because of these certainties, playing dumb was the only safe response.

"Listen!" the officer commanded. He paused for a sweeping survey of the men and women before him. "We are here to keep you informed of the guerrilla activities." He held his rolled-up paper like a riding crop. "We have information that the Communists are going to enter this area. Perhaps they have already come." He waved the cone, and a soldier pulled old Señora Catú toward the center.

A fearful murmur rose up but died instantly. If something awful happened to her, nothing could be done. Isabel prayed softly that Señora Catú would not be harmed. The old woman trembled visibly as she was forced toward the officer.

"Go ahead," he commanded.

The woman dared not look up. She spoke hollowly, barely audibly. "Our steer was killed by the guerrillas."

The officer signaled for her to be released. It was meant only for show, as independent testimony.

"All of you know this. Fortunately, Juan Catú was not in his field when they came, or surely they would have butchered him as they butchered the animal. You people must protect yourselves against these Communists. They are people with no morals, no dignity. They want to use the people of the fields to bring bloodshed to all of Guatemala. They do not care about you. To them, you are bodies to be sacrificed for their own greed. They want only to destroy.

"They want you to give up your lands, the lands your ancestors farmed. They want to put all the fields into the hands of their government. These people will divide up your father's property and your grandfather's property and give it to someone from the coast, or the Petén. Someone who has never lived here, someone who doesn't know the customs and doesn't care that the Tzutujiles fought bravely against the Quiché and Cakchiquel to give his half of the lake to their children and their children's children.

"They want to take away your clothes and give you the clothes of the ladino. None of you will own anything. What your forefathers gave, they will take away. They will say 'no' to your beliefs and they will say that to believe in God is wrong, that there is no God. They will crush your church, stamp out your shrines. *Sanjorín* and priest will be killed. The pews will be burned. Your shrines in the hills and mountains will be desecrated and destroyed.''

The officer unrolled his cone and read to himself before again rolling up the paper.

"They will kill anyone who believes that God is supreme. You must worship their government instead. Their government will be your only god. To disobey them is to die. Already they have entered the area. The woman has seen what they do. Count yourselves lucky that you did not see them because if you had, that would have been the last thing you saw. Count yourself lucky that this woman and this man escaped.'' He referred to the paper again. "Go home tonight and give thanks to God that you did not see them.'' He passed the cone to a guard and watched as the soldier taped it to the center of the stone cross.

"I will address the men now,'' the officer continued. "The Communists want to enter. We will not let them enter. Henceforth, there will be a civil patrol. Five men will take watch and patrol the paths and highways. You will carry clubs and machetes. Do not carry any weapon. No hunting rifle. No guns. The Communists have weapons. Farmers have only sticks and machetes. That is what you will carry. Questions?''

He did not bother to see if there were any. "Nicolás Cauec,'' he said, ordering the mayor forward. The mayor inched out from the circle of people and stood several feet away from the officer.

"Captain,'' he said.

"Men between the ages of seventeen and fifty will take turns.''

Isabel felt José tense up beside her.

"No one is to be excused. Those who refuse to be a part of the patrol refuse to help Guatemala. They are enemies of the people. They do not want to fight against Guatemala's enemies. The man who does not patrol has chosen which side he wishes to die on. This has only two sides. Do you understand?"

"Yes."

"Are there any problems?"

"No, Captain."

"We will stay two days to show you how it is done."

"Yes, Captain."

The officer's eyes confidently swept the faces again. His gaze finished on the mayor. "I want the name of every man. You and your council will meet with me now." He turned and walked between his guards and into the church.

Nicolás watched him. He took a step forward and stopped. One guard followed the captain. The other two drew closer to the mayor. Nicolás turned to the audience, searching for the appropriate faces. The six council members pulled awkwardly away from the wall of watchers.

Isabel felt José shift beside her, but her eyes were on the men who walked forlornly toward the church. She kept her attention on the guards moving warily alongside Nicolás, even when she felt José touch her arm. His hand spun her away from the scene, and she stood staring not at José, but at the young man she had seen butchering the steer. She squealed. The young man tightened his grip on her elbow. His grip and intense eyes held her transfixed, unable to move or breathe or think.

"Go home," he said softly, his tone full of warning. When she did not budge, his expression turned to stone. "Go home!"

Isabel looked around. She should read the notice for her father. Around her, most of the villagers hurried down the path to their homes. A few cast glances at her and the soldier. José stood several feet away, imploring her with every muscle in his face to do as the soldier said, to not say anything, to obey, obey, obey. She turned to the young man again. He repeated the same two words, with absolute detachment, pretending he had never seen her before. "Go home!"

She backed away, confused yet certain the truth about this man would never be known to her.

Twelve

To Maria's surprise, her father wanted to make the trip to Sololá. He searched out Allan Waters and asked him to help. Without saying as much, he had had enough of Eziquel Coxol, she thought.

The morning of the trip, Alfredo drew the line on who would go. José and Diego complained, as did Marcelina, but they finally understood that each person would cost three more quetzales, and that was only if the family took along food to save on that expense.

Allan Waters waited at the doorway and listened to the Tzutujil. He didn't need to understand the exact words to know that this was probably a conversation like most conversations between parents and children all over the world. "I'll pay for everyone," he offered.

Isabel saw her father's pride begin to rise to the defense.

"Please," Allan said diplomatically. "I have caused so much trouble that it seems a good way for me to make amends."

When Alfredo consented, the boys cuffed each other in their excitement.

The first bus going toward Santiago came early enough to get them to the six o'clock boat to Panajachel. All seven boarded the dark and nearly empty bus. It had come from the capital, its final leg the unpaved road between San Lucas Tolimán and Santiago Atitlán. Those few going from terminus to terminus tried their best to get what limited sleep they could on the extremely bumpy road. The Pacays stared with relief as Allan paid the half quetzal for each of them. Perhaps out of habit, not one of them fully believed that the trip wouldn't take precious money away from them. They rocked and lurched through predawn.

Once in Santiago, they descended to the docks. There was one foreigner waiting for the same boat. The short, bearded man sat in the grass, away from the docks, and wrote in a fat red book. His glasses looked awkward on his hooked nose. Isabel had a curious desire to run up to the funny man and see what it was he scribbled: What language did he write in? Did he feel as much a stranger in Santiago as she did? Where was he off to? From where did he come?

Allan Waters talked to Alfredo about his experience with the boats. He had made an unpleasant trip in late June, during the festival of the patron saint of San Pedro la Laguna. "It was the *Santa María*," he said.

Alfredo explained that all boats to San Pedro from

131

Santiago were owned by the same person and that no one liked him.

"I had been working here for two months," Allan continued, "and the man wanted to charge me two quetzales instead of the usual seventy-five centavos."

"You're a foreigner."

"But he didn't charge the Mexicans or the Spaniards and they were more tourists than I am. I'm working here. I rent a room here. Besides, he was very rude. My friends tried to tell him that I was not a tourist, that I had been working and living in Santiago, but he was just rude. He wouldn't listen to anyone."

Isabel saw that Allan Waters was not gaining great sympathy from her father. She recalled Allan's leather pack and expensive camera. He could easily afford the two quetzales, which was much less than an American dollar.

"They finally took one quetzal from me and told me that I would have to pay two from now on. They told me not to come back. So that's why I'll never go back to San Pedro. I tell everyone to watch out for the owner of the *Santa María*. He's too arrogant. Not at all like the people of the *Jucán Ya*."

"The boat we're taking this morning?" Isabel asked.

"Yes. Those people are very friendly. And fair. They always talk to me and ask how I'm doing. Because of their friendliness, I only take their boats to Panajachel."

Alfredo helped Manuela sit in the grass to wait.

"How long does it take?" asked José.

"About an hour."

Three other foreigners arrived as the boat made the

bend into the inlet. When the foreigners got closer, Isabel realized that one of them was not a woman, as she had first thought, but a man. She giggled at his clothing, particularly the pants, which had swatches of women's skirts from different regions of Guatemala. His shirt was a *huipil,* and his hair hung in tight braids past his shoulders. He wore earrings as well. Manuela would not believe that it was not a woman no matter how much Isabel insisted. They both stared and chuckled behind their hands. For the first time in many days, Isabel saw her mother change back into the person she remembered in love with her father and someone with a sense of humor as well.

"It's a woman," Alfredo said flatly, confidently.

The foreigner reached out and put an arm around a woman waring a tight black skirt that revealed half of her thighs. They kissed and nuzzled.

"It's a man," Alfredo said flatly, confidently.

All of them could hardly keep from laughing out loud. The foreigners knew they were being watched. Isabel turned to see the bearded foreigner watching both groups, his pen poised above his book.

"Wait till you see Panajachel," Allan whispered.

Isabel pressed him.

"You'll see foreigners in stranger clothes than that. You won't even know that you're in Guatemala. Everything is foreign. Americans, particularly, have made the place like parts of the States. You'll see people from all over the world who want to pretend that they're in another country. I like to say that it's the perfect place where foreigners can convince themselves they've left their country, without really having left it. Many of them also think that being poor is special, so they try to act as if they're as poor as the people who live here. They don't understand that they, luckily, will never be so poor."

"Why would they do something so stupid?" Alfredo asked.

Allan turned his palms heavenward. "I have no idea at all. It's a kind of game, maybe."

Marcelina couldn't understand this horrible place. "Then why are we going?"

"We have to go through Panajachel to get to Solá."

At six, they piled into the large white boat. The boys sat in the open back. The others sat together inside the cabin. The bearded foreigner sat in the back of the cabin; the other foreigners lounged on top of the boat. Isabel and her mother snickered as they watched the strangely dressed trio disappear up the side. One hairy foot hung in the window for a moment. It wore a leather sandal, like that of richer peasants, and a silver bracelet around the ankle.

"Woman," Alfredo proclaimed.

Manuela shook her head.

Dawn had burned away most of the fog except for clumps that still floated above languorous eddies along the shoreline. Isabel watched small boats suddenly appear from these fogbanks and glide across the still lake. The fishermen stood as they oared into view. They seemed like dream figures emerging from the obscure veil of the subconscious to coast out in clear light. And like dream figures, they emerged with trails of fog: Some wisps came trolling in their soft wakes; others were snagged on the roughly hewn gunwales; some clung to the men's bodies and clothes like tatters of ghostly robes.

"It's beautiful in the morning," Allan said to her.

Isabel nodded, her gaze taking in the shoreline, the inlets, the fishermen moving out, and the great wall of volcanoes imprisoning the lake. She looked at the people in the cabin. Many were trying to sleep; others conversed quietly. Her mother's eyes were closed. Her father stared straight ahead at the white door of the cabin.

The boat slipped free of the inlet and entered the wide expanse of the lake. It lurched forward as the engine dug deep into water. Most conversations dropped off; two men spoke above the noise, but they talked about nothing private. Isabel held her mother close and allowed herself to doze, her head resting against her mother's head.

Midway through the lulling voyage, Isabel opened her eyes. Her family still dozed. Allan Waters leaned against the seat in front of him and cradled his head in his arms. Nearly everyone slept. Those who didn't stared dreamily out. Isabel looked up at the northern mountains. The range above the village of Tzununá took shape in her imagination. She noticed that the peaks and slopes formed a man's face looking straight up to the heavens. The man had a moustache and broad forehead, like the face of a Spaniard or a foreigner. The slightly parted lips made this enormous face seem to be in some private and intense reverie while looking up to the sky. She dozed again under the rocking of the boat, the white noise of the engine, and the image of a giant foreigner beseeching the heavens.

* * *

They drank coffee and ate bread at a stand on the beach. Manuela stared with amazement at the number of foreigners, most dressed in only somewhat less bizarre clothing than the man–woman on the boat. A row of restaurants extended the length of the road above the beach. Each one had a scattering of foreigners, some eating, most merely watching or reading. Allan smiled knowingly.

Isabel saw the recognition of wealth on her father's face.

As if recognizing the look, too, Allan made a noise in his throat and said, "Most of them don't want to spend money. They want to have everything as cheap as they can. The Europeans are the worst. They think that paying a poor Guatemalan next to nothing for his work means they have experienced the country more than those who spend more money. It's a strange idea, but one that a great many foreigners believe."

They walked up the road, past the Hotel del Lago and small cafés with luxurious patios. Cakchiquel women, carrying loads of odd shirts and pants, approached every foreigner to aggressively sell. Girls carried cardboard placards covered with cloth-and-bead bracelets. Everywhere the wares were the same. And all of it was an ugly mixture of traditional colors and patterns with utterly foreign designs.

Manuela actually walked fairly quickly up the road to catch a minivan to Sololá. She hardly looked at the foreigners dressed like caricatures of Mayas, their patchwork clothes showing little respect or regard for the regional traditions they were jumbling together. The foreigners who dressed in the worst mockery of Guatemala were also the ones selling jewelry alongside Indians who were trying to earn a living from tourism. She groaned as an older woman and man passed quickly by the desperate Mayan stalls to look happily at jewelry made by foreigners for foreign tastes.

Allan Waters seemed to understand Manuela perfectly. He walked with a frown. "I hate these people who hang on here," he said, not really caring who heard him and more interested in venting his anger than in carrying on a dialogue with any of the Pacays. "These people cause more damage than they realize. And they think that they're somehow more spiritual or closer to Guatemalans by acting like this. They not only steal part of the market from the natives, but they ruin the traditions by forcing rapid changes."

Isabel saw that he was earnest, though he seemed to have no idea that he had also barged in where he wasn't wanted and had expected to bring his customs to a place besieged by a changing world.

Allan continued without anyone commenting. "When foreigners come here, they naturally like the things that these foreigners make more than they like the traditional things. After all, they're from the same culture and their sense of beauty is similar. So what happens is that the natives have to change their styles to compete." His arm swept outward, taking in all of the street. "And this is the result. Try and find anything traditional here. You can't. All of this is either ladino or foreign! They have dozens of pizza and hamburger restaurants, for God's sake. Even a movie theatre owned by a Texan. It's all gone to hell!''

"Pizza?" José said, working the word between his tongue and teeth.

"If they want to have all the comforts of home, why the hell don't they stay home?"

Alfredo looked at Allan with something like new appreciation. He clearly didn't know what to make of this bellowing young man. Allan certainly had no clue as to the contradictions in his behavior, and he spoke as if he were speaking to himself, not to them, but there was something in his naïve energy that made him endearing—and something in his naïve ranting that made him an ally.

Manuela walked as best she could, like a grand lady hobbling up the street, without a glance at the misfortunes around her. The boys and Marcelina watched everything, and everything to them was gloriously new. Isabel helped her mother as she too tried to figure out whether Allan Waters told the truth or simply connived to make them like him. She looked where his arms pointed and saw the ridiculous costumes of the foreigners and the completely altered Mayan clothing. She saw Cakchiqueles and Tzutujiles selling in the streets as well. All of their marketed clothing was identical. And they had an anxiousness or a jadedness about them that the foreign vendors didn't. She could not imagine the Mayas selling so many identical bracelets, shirts, and skirts no matter how many rich foreigners came as tourists. And yet there were more white people in Panajachel than she ever could have thought possible. Perhaps these things really did sell.

"Look at that!" Allan said with contempt.

An open restaurant was filled with foreigners in tattered clothes, many of them young women with children on their laps, all of them eating beans and tortillas. Above the restaurant a sign read EL PSICODÉLICO.

"Those are the true natives of Panajachel, not the Cakchiqueles!"

Isabel felt relieved when they reached the top of the street, though she could not take her eyes off the seemingly thousands of foreigners milling about or waiting alongside enormous backpacks for buses to Antigua. José gawked openly at the women blatantly wearing only small panties and bras in the streets. Some, in perverse imitation of the Mayan shawl, or so he thought, wore beach towels around their necks. Thankfully, a van came quickly and took them up the winding road to Sololá.

They waited patiently in the green metal chairs. Allan Waters paced. Manuela again silently refused to look at her surroundings—once again because everything smacked of dying. Only here, in the hospital, it was a physical dying. The smell in the hallway made her crinkle her nose and spit. It had taken all of them several minutes to persuade her not to turn away from the pale green walls and go immediately home to die. They had, in fact, nearly given up the battle of persuasion when a young Tzutujil woman from San Lucas

139

came out with her husband and new child and tipped the scale to their side. They compromised.

"I won't wait more than an hour," she declared.

Once inside, Allan paced through each minute until it seemed certain that the hour would come and go and everything he had hoped to gain for them and for himself would simply dissolve away. He plopped down beside Alfredo. His blond head dipped into his large hands.

"What did the doctor say?" Alfredo asked. He had asked the same question every ten minutes since Allan had returned from a room with a wire-mesh window.

"That it would be soon," he abbreviated from his crouch.

Marcelina curled tighter into Isabel's lap.

Then Allan's head came up with a "Thank you for coming." His expression was one of contrition. "I thought I could do something for you."

Alfredo smiled at the young man.

"My father lived in Guatemala many years ago."

"Really?"

"He was a doctor. He died a few years ago."

"Was he very old?"

Allan had to think in terms of Alfredo's world and Manuela's illness. "No."

"I see."

"He died of a heart attack." Allan looked reflexively at Manuela. "He didn't exercise very much, even though he was always very active. He traveled all through Central America on medical projects."

"Like you," Alfredo said.

"Well, like I want to someday. I guess part of me

140

wants to go around and take medicine to people who can't get any." He looked into Alfredo's face. "But maybe there are people who don't want me to bring them anything."

Isabel stared at her feet.

"Maybe things are difficult for some people," Alfredo explained. He was beginning to like this American Waters. "People's lives are not usually so simple as you may think."

Allan's face brightened under Alfredo's warm advice. "All I want is to help people get treatment. I don't want to change anything. Really. I respect what people have. But there are other ways, too. Why not have several opportunities?" In his excitement, his Spanish took on the flavor of literal English translation. "Why not be able to seek help in different ways? Why not?" He stopped, his hands pointing at Alfredo.

Alfredo only smiled.

Allan shrugged, yet he saw Isabel listening with interest, her face giving him back something of hope, something that said he wasn't just ranting. He opened his mouth to speak when her face turned upward to look past him.

The doctor motioned. "Not everyone," he said, when all seven stepped forward.

José herded Diego and Marcelina back into the chairs. Isabel moved back to her seat, too, but her father told her to come with her mother.

The room had two large bookcases filled with fat reference books, a brown patient's bed, a sink, and a cabinet with tall jars of sticks and cotton on the top level. Under the top counter, cigar-shaped probes, scissors, and trays were arranged in neat rows. The doctor instructed Isabel to lead Manuela to sit on the table. Alfredo sat in a chair opposite the doctor. Isabel and Allan stood against the wall. The doctor listened to the symptoms, all the time caressing the silver head of the stethoscope that hung around his neck. He nodded and stroked until he felt he had heard enough from Isabel and Alfredo.

"I need to give her a physical," he said. When the others made no move, he explained: "She'll have to take off her *huipil.*"

Manuela raised her eyes for the first time.

The doctor bowed slightly to Alfredo. "Perhaps your daughter wants to remain with her mother."

Allan left. Alfredo followed mechanically, hesitating at the door to look at his frightened wife. Isabel sat beside her on the thickly padded table.

"She'll be all right," the doctor said. "Don't worry."

When he turned back to the two women, they were huddled together and as far against the wall as they could get while sitting on the table.

"It's nothing," the doctor said. He approached with his stethoscope disk held out. "I'm just going to listen to your heart."

Manuela's hands clutched Isabel's arm.

The doctor put the ends of the instrument into his ears and brought the disk up in front of him as he stepped close. Now both of the women wrapped into each other's arms.

The doctor chuckled kindly. "Come on," he said. "Haven't you ever seen one of these? It won't hurt. Here. I'll show you. I'll put it here. This is where I'll put it on you. See: Nothing happens. All I want to do is listen. Let me show you." He tried to put the ear-pieces into Manuela's ears, but she drew back with a threatening glare. Isabel decided she had better accept the instrument or all would be lost. First she heard the doctor's heart thumping, then, with surprised laughter, her own heart.

"Brum-bumb," she said in imitation.

The doctor laughed with her. "Listen to your mother."

Isabel placed the disk at the top of her mother's *huipil*, at the throat.

"Lower."

She brought the disk down an inch.

"Now let me hear."

He listened intently for a moment, then gave it back to Isabel. "Hold it against her back. No, under the blouse."

Isabel listened again.

"Hold the disk and let me hear." They shifted the stethoscope and he listened much longer. With his hand over the blouse and on top of Isabel's, he guided the disk to several points on her back. "Okay, take it out." He held the disk in his fingers and moved it to just under the front of Manuela's blouse. "Please?" he asked.

Manuela closed her eyes as the doctor pressed the stethoscope between her breasts.

The others waited in the hallway without a word. Allan expected a barrage of questions from Alfredo, but the older man sat stiffly and silently, keeping his privacy tightly bound. The minutes passed with no change in Alfredo or his children, until finally the door opened.

Both men hurried inside to find Manuela standing with her arms crossed and an adamant glare on her face.

Isabel raised her eyebrows. "He wants to take her blood to do some test," she explained.

"That's normal," Allan said.

The doctor settled into his cushioned chair. "She refuses all tests."

"But you have to," Allan pleaded. "That's why we came. He can't tell what you have without tests."

"I told her that."

Allan turned to him. "Is there any other way?"

"Everything points to bacterial endocarditis. She's had rheumatic fever, or at least there's a high chance of her having had it. There are residual nodules in her joints. Frequent nosebleeds as a child. Involuntary twitching and memorable 'growing pains.' What concerns me is the possibility of rheumatic heart condition and the increased likelihood of coronary occlusion as a result. She seems to have the classic symptoms: nocturnal dyspnea, angina, dizziness, fatigue. She could have started with congenital valve abnormalities. Her parents never went to a doctor."

Not one of them, even Allan Waters, pretended to understand this litany of strange sounds. Yet only Allan followed enough to get to the important question: "What should she do?"

"Have tests."

Manuela tightened her crossed arms.

"If it is bacterial endocarditis, it's very easy to care for. If it isn't, what I recommend might do her more harm. The only sensible thing is to have tests."

"No," Manuela said.

144

"But why?" the doctor asked. "You've come this far. Why not have the tests?"

"No."

"I'll pay for the trip," Allan pleaded. "I'll pay for the tests. Please."

Isabel looked for the answer from Alfredo, then at her mother, who stood resolute.

"I'll pay for the medicine."

Manuela walked to her husband and tugged his sleeve until he followed her out. Isabel dutifully followed.

Allan saw his chance moving out the door. "Wait," he said.

Isabel stopped and turned.

"Meet me tomorrow at the soccer field."

She saw him again as a boy, earnest and well meaning. "Okay. At three." And she left.

Allan didn't know what to say to the doctor. What he was trying to do seemed so futile. Perhaps he really didn't know enough to be taking on such a project. He would have to hurry, too, to catch up with the family.

The doctor waited in his chair.

"I'm sorry," Allan said.

"Never mind. When they get sick, all their neighbors come and tell them what to do. The neighbors will give them a folk remedy that someone used in such and such place. When that doesn't work, then they use the healers. Only a small percentage come here and usually with the idea that all hope is gone. To them, this is a step closer to the grave, Mr. Waters. They'd prefer to die at home, not here under the care of ladinos like me. If nothing else, dying at home eases the financial burden on the family." He stood to show Allan out.

"Funny, I don't know what research has been done on folk medicine. I mean the pharmacology of folk remedies. I wish I knew. Some of them work. Some remedies are as old as the Maya. They've passed the test of time. But some are pure—"

Allan stopped him. "Can I buy the medicine?"

The doctor pushed a hand through his hair. When he finally spoke, his voice was quiet with thought. "Those who live in cities go to the drugstore and buy whatever they want. That's part of the reason dental problems are so bad. Too many wide-spectrum antibiotics. They take them like aspirin, when they can find them. Those who want more, get more. Any drug they want. Penicillin, opiates. Anything. Does it surprise you? Not at all like the United States, is it?" He smirked. "You ask about my medical ethics? Should a doctor give medicine without proper diagnosis? You should ask. Well, this is not the United States." The doctor shifted on his feet, settled his weight, dug his hands deep into his pockets. "Okay," he said. "I'll get it for you."

Thirteen

When Isabel saw the new warning by their door, she knew she really would go see Allan Waters. Her family had stood by the gate on their return from Sololá, looking down at the circle of pine and candles and, this time, the claw of a hen. 'See!'' was all that Manuela had said. It was all she felt she needed to say, as if the new spell vindicated her resolution in Sololá. She walked wide around the sign, as if it carried immediate danger, giving it the greatest respect as she dragged Marcelina with her into the house.

Isabel was relieved that her father told her to help him clean up. She had so many questions, starting with the obvious.

"I don't know who's doing this," he answered distractedly. He picked up the claw and tossed it far out into the brush on the other side of the avenue. "I suppose they didn't want us to go to Sololá."

"Because of Allan Waters?"

"Hm. Yes."

Isabel held the gathered pine in her arms. "Would Eziquel do such a thing?"

"Maybe several people are doing this." He brushed aside needles with the side of his foot. "No one wants us to seek help from the American or from the doctors. Didn't the women come here? Didn't they say this to you?" His foot scraped another small pile of needles. "No, Isabel, I don't know who's behind these things."

"What about Mami?"

"Please," he said, as if it were an old argument too full of history to even begin discussing with her. "Let's go to sleep."

"But why doesn't she want the medicine?"

Alfredo walked toward the door without answering. The pillar of his body said that he would not discuss it.

Yet Isabel would not quit so easily. "Will you talk to her? Please, Papa?"

Alfredo turned in the doorway. The inside oil lamp gave him a crippled silhouette. He nodded tiredly, his shadowed head dipping slowly, his arms dangling awkwardly.

"I'll try, Isabel. I'll try. But don't think much will change."

The next day, she anxiously awaited afternoon to hear what hope Allan Waters might pass to her. In his words would lie secreted some way to help her mother. Of that she was sure. Thus, when the hour arrived, she

148

hurried to the soccer field, walking through the foot-paths in fields rather than the more visible avenues of Chuuí Chopaló. She had to pass the school, but she did so at a good run.

Allan sat waiting on the short wall behind the far goal. He stood when she came near. "I'm glad you came. I thought maybe you wouldn't."

She felt shy, awkward. "I have come."

"Yes." He smiled. "You have come."

Isabel sat on the wall and folded her hands into her lap.

"How is your mother?"

"Like a stone."

Allan didn't understand.

"She refuses help."

He sat beside her; his hand reached down for something to hold and came back up with a curving brown twig. "She needs to have the tests, you know."

"What will they do?"

"Well, I'm not sure." He gathered up his best Spanish. "Blood tests might reveal bacterial infection, I suppose. Maybe they would show cholesterol in her blood. Perhaps they would show other problems. X rays and the other things will probably show the condition of her heart, but I'm not really sure, Isabel."

"And what are all those things?"

"X rays? Blood tests? Cholesterol?"

"The last one."

"Well, it's . . . Funny, no one has ever asked me that before. I don't know how to explain it. In the States, everyone talks about it as if we all know what it is. Fat deposits in the blood. Yes, something like that.

Fat in the blood that clogs the veins, makes the heart work too hard, and then it can lead to heart attack."

"That's what the doctor was afraid of, wasn't it? He said she has a chance of having an attack."

Allan nodded.

"What does that mean?"

"She could die." He wanted to sound grim, holding, as he thought, the obvious solution. "But he also said that it's easy to take care of her illness, Isabel. If he knew for certain what she has, it would be easy for her to get better."

"I know."

"But he has to know for certain."

"I know."

"You need to convince her."

"I know!"

Allan drew back. His own hands collapsed into one another between his knees. "I'm sorry," he said. "I talk too much. I say dumb things. I know you know. It's just hard for me to understand why she won't do it."

Isabel couldn't resist: "I know."

They both smiled.

Isabel sighed heavily. "Look, it's more than just being afraid of the doctor or the hospital. It's you, too. We don't ask for people to come here and investigate. What are they investigating, anyway? We're people. We have lived here a very long time without Americans or your doctors. We have lived here before there were any foreigners. Every foreigner wants to take something. Well, what do they give to us?"

"Help."

"They give what they think we need, not what we ask to receive. Don't you see that?"

"I guess so."

"It's like what you told us in Sololá. What did you say about those people in Panajachel? Those heppies, you called them."

"Hippies. I see your point."

"They come and want to be like the people here, but they can never be like we are. They will return to their—how did you say it?—safe lives. Or they have special freedom to know the world. In the end, all they do is take our things. When they try to give us something, even that is just another way to take."

"Like the jewelry," Allan muttered. "Or the clothing."

"Like the medicine."

"I see."

"The ladino is not the Indian, Allan Waters."

"No, I know that."

"And perhaps you need to know that the ladino is very racist. To the ladino, we aren't even human. But the saddest thing is that the Indian thinks he is worse than all the others, that it's bad to be an Indian because this is what he has been told to believe since he was a little boy. Every day more Indians want to be like the ladino."

"I didn't know that."

"In Santiago you can see it. Look at the way they dress. Some men wear very embroidered pants to show they're from the upper class of Indians. They want to show they are not poor Indians. Some have already stopped wearing traditional clothes. But here in Chuuí

151

Chopaló not many are like that." Isabel ended with a pride that surprised even her. It felt as if she were finally understanding things for herself by having to explain. By giving voice to the ideas lodged like dormant seeds in her mind, the ideas sprouted and grew and took form for her as well: "My father has seen everything ending for so long," she whispered. "He has known this for so long."

Allan looked questioningly at her, but she gazed at the ground before her, lost in something he would never hear about.

Her face and voice suddenly lifted with new understanding. "What he did for me . . ." And just as fast, her voice trailed back into that internal privacy, that guarded silence.

"*¿Como?*" asked Allan.

"Nothing." She looked into the shallow blue of his eyes, believing that those eyes could understand little of anything old and traditional and different from the world into which they were born. Those eyes of dead fish.

"Nothing?"

Isabel gave herself a quick shake. "My mother is not like my father," she proclaimed. "She doesn't want to see anything disappear. She wants to be like a rock." Her voice dropped back into that inner well: "Poor Papa. He wants to think there might be something good in change."

"There is!" Allan was on his feet.

Isabel, however, sat patiently, almost wearily. "You *don't* understand."

"What?"

"It's not that simple."

"I'm sorry. I'm trying. I really am."

"You are not simply you in Chuuí Chopaló," she explained. "You are an American. The doctor is not a doctor to us; he is a ladino. The medicine is not medicine." Isabel felt her voice rising. "It's a piece of something else—of, well, of losing! It is something from your world entering my mother's belly! Don't you see what that means? It is something that will be inside her forever, growing there." Isabel felt angry, not at him, but because she had not understood it herself until now, until speaking in her mother's defense, until seeing her mother's side of things. "That is what her illness means!" Now *she* was on her feet, upset for having missed it all until this moment.

She looked out across the soccer field, out to the horizons, as if to cast her new understanding like a net across all of her people's land. To her amazement, Lucas stood at the other side of the field, observing her and Allan. It jolted her, transfixed her to the ground. She hadn't seen him before. And then she thought he would come and join them, but he remained where he was. She did not know what to do or say. Lucas and she stared at each other.

His face suddenly reddened with such emotion that it drew out his name from Isabel's throat. She wanted that expression—that bitterness on his face—to end. He walked furiously toward them, stepping within shoving distance of Allan, and rocked him back with the flat of his hand against the taller man's chest.

Isabel shouted, "No!"

"Wait a minute," Allan said. His hands were out in

front of him, palms up. "What's going on?" His Spanish instantly became worse than ever.

Lucas insulted him in Tzutujil.

Isabel moved between them. "What are you doing? Are you crazy?"

"What are *you* doing?" he demanded back.

"Talking about my mother!"

"Your mother?"

"Yes! He's trying to help. At least he cares about my mother. And that's more than you do!"

"So it's true?"

"What's the problem?" asked Allan. "What do you think is going on?"

Lucas faced him again. "Get away from me, *gringo!*"

"Hey! What the hell's the matter with you?"

"Weren't you told to leave?"

Allan stepped closer, more confidently. "Isabel asked me to come here."

Lucas turned red again. He glared at Isabel as if to fill her eyes with the shame he thought she should have. And then his mouth contorted with barely reined hatred: "Whore!" he called her.

Isabel's legs buckled.

Lucas spun on his heels and walked furiously away.

No sound would come from Isabel's throat.

"Hey!" Allan shouted. "Hey!" Lucas paid no attention. Allan reached instead to comfort Isabel, but she pulled away from him as if he were diseased, pockmarked, something wicked.

She ran.

"Wait!"

She would not stop, and he ran after her. "I have

the medicine for your mother. Don't go!" Midway down the field, he blocked her way and thrust the medicine into her hands. Three colored bottles fell to the ground. Allan grabbed her arms and shook her.

She cried out in anguish.

"Listen! I don't know what's wrong with him. Listen! If he's jealous, he's wrong."

Isabel looked into his handsome face with new shame. It had crossed her mind; she could not lie to herself about it.

"Lucas is wrong! That's all there is to it. Don't let that stop you from helping your mother. Take the medicine. Try to get her to take it. You have to try."

She felt the energy fall from her and her body filling to overflowing with sadness.

Allan gathered up the bottles and formed her limp hands into a cup to receive the medicine. "Take them. The doctor wrote instructions. Please. It's all very simple."

Isabel slowly focused on her hands.

He picked out the green bottle. "She needs to take one of these every day." He picked out the brown bottle. "She needs to take one every day. It's easy, see. You can't get confused." And the white bottle last. He opened it and took out a capsule wrapped in a net. "Listen to me. Are you listening?"

Isabel stared blankly at the capsule.

"If she is having a bad spell, break this in your hand and let her smell it." He quickly opened the other bottles and stuck them under her eyes. "See how different they are. It's easy, Isabel. See?" He pretended to crush the capsule between his fingers and then waved it under her nose. "Like this. Are you listening? Do you see?"

Isabel took the bottles. She put them in a plastic bag Allan fished out from his pocket, and she moved woodenly out of the field.

"Don't forget," he called behind her, "I'm above the Restaurant Susy. Get me if I can help! Don't forget!"

But he knew that no one would come to him for help. Isabel did not even turn. He knew that it would be the end of his work in Chuuí Chopaló unless some miracle happened. It was finished for him. He looked at his hands as if to see the prescription bottles yet cradled in his palm. "Oh, man," he whispered, "what have I done?"

Fourteen

Isabel had never felt so alone in all her life. Everything had collapsed around her without her knowing why or when the crumbling into ruins had begun. Her mother, worse now than ever, should have been brought closer to health by the trip to Sololá and by the medicine Isabel now held in a plastic bag within her shawl. Instead, Manuela's wall of refusal, like the walls of the ancient city of Oro Hill, served not to protect her from diseased and corrupting forces but to isolate her and to guarantee a predictable end. If she would simply submit, then she would live. But her mother's decision was final.

At the base of this refusal, Isabel's own future, her vision of teaching, lay broken. Also shut out was Alfredo's dream for his children, his family. All of them lay besieged by the calamity and by her mother's refusal to consider possibilities. But this refusal was one demanded by the forces of the village itself.

Isabel felt the worst symptom of this ending lay in the deterioration of her relationship with Lucas. So much was in ruin, so much in a private desperation, that Isabel became convinced that everything—her mother's illness, the signs at the house, the angry *sanjorín,* Lucas's final word to her—all of it was entirely her fault. She had caused it all by thinking selfishly, by turning away from what was expected of her, by being convinced that she could be an exception to the volcanic forces that smelted people into acceptable molds.

All that remained for her was the powerful desire to erase the past few weeks. She wanted to obliterate all that had happened and embrace completely the task of being a selfless woman, a tireless mother to her siblings, an obedient wife to Lucas. She saw how easy it could be. How natural it could seem. It was what the world told her to be. Everything would be simple and as it was meant to be. All she needed to do was embrace that, to concede, to give up—and then with chagrin, she thought that that was exactly what her mother had to do, what she was demanding of her mother: this giving in.

But something inside her hated this comparison. Isabel felt a strangeness over the comparison that became a muscle pang in her stomach. It was not the same! There *was* something different—yet doubt is an imp that needles and deceives from within.

She left her home at a dead run and went up the hill toward school, her mind in a boil of questions that had no easy answers: Why did Lucas come to the field?

158

How had he known Isabel and Allan were there? Why had Lucas been so angry? Why had he called her a whore? What was he hearing? And why wasn't the giving up that society demanded of her the same as what she was asking of her mother?

Isabel arrived breathless at the top of the road and sat on a bank overlooking the school yard. Her only certainty was that Maestro Xiloj might unravel her confusion. She arrived prepared to sit for hours until school ended and Maestro Xiloj came up the path to return to his home in Santiago. However, the students began appearing long before the normal hour. Her friends left the classrooms, stood awhile in groups, and descended to their homes without a glance at her, or glancing with a flurry of whispers to one another. She did not want to think about them or their malicious whispering. She tried deliberately not to think of them, to erase their petty haranguing from her mind. She did not want even to understand why they were all leaving so early. All of these things threatened to steal energy from her purpose. She wanted to hold her tumble of questions tightly, keep them together like a bright object, a compact ball, in her mind's eye and to take it out when Maestro Xiloj appeared. She wanted to pass the bewildering object to him and listen to his wise unraveling.

Below her, the teachers began gathering, too. They stood for a time in a small clutch, shaking one another's hands with strange solemnity. The brightness of Isabel's ball dimmed as she watched them. Through that dimming came the inevitable idea that something serious was going on. Maestro Xiloj looked dark and unhappy, his face in shadows. And when the teachers walked up the hill and toward the road to catch the bus, the sobriety of their manner brought her to her feet. She felt as if she were watching a funeral march. Suddenly, absurdly, she thought that her mother had died. Yet it couldn't be. She had just left her mother. She had just been with her and no matter what other injustices existed, death would not come so quickly. Surely her mother would be safe in the house. Surely.

Andrés Xiloj noticed her pale and frightened expression. The smile he forced only succeeded in worrying her more.

"What's the matter?" she asked, still harboring an illogical fear of her mother's death.

He separated from the others. "The teachers have called a strike." And because he saw that she still did not understand, he explained. "All teachers are going to stop work until the government agrees to have better student lunches and to pay rural teachers higher salaries."

From out of the fog of her own concerns, she recalled when the school, months earlier, stopped giving tortillas and beans for lunch and began giving each student one small package of crackers and a small cup of sugar water.

"Our petitions have been answered, finally. But they refused to give any money to education." His hands fanned outward. "We said we would strike if they answered this way. So here we are."

Isabel shook her head. This was like a terrible joke; it was incomprehensible. "When . . . Why didn't I know about this?"

Xiloj smiled sympathetically. "You've had other

problems, Isabel. Anyway, most people didn't know until today. Many of us, myself included, thought that it wouldn't get this far. We thought our petition would be answered in a different way.''

''But what about the school? What will you do?''

''Go home. Write letters for support. March.''

Isabel struggled to understand it all, but her body felt as if it were someone else's, her mind hanging just out of reach, her heart thumping elsewhere. It was as if she had suddenly awakened and found herself dislocated in time. She felt alienated from everything, so that her own concerns began to take on an unreal quality.

Xiloj continued, prompted by her bewilderment. ''The different districts will take turns marching in the capital until we get an audience with the president. With luck, it won't take long. We have to try.''

So life continued without her. She began to feel ashamed for thinking that she was the center of anything. The dislocation turned into a feeling of smallness, of stupidity. She felt powerless. Like a child again.

''I'm sorry,'' he said. He rubbed her shoulders. He tried to read the confusion in her face. ''This will affect everyone, you know?''

''Oh'' was all that bubbled from her mouth.

''Some of you have already suffered. Like you. I know what you've been going through. I know it feels like there's no fairness.''

Isabel's gaze dropped in assent.

''Maybe there isn't.'' The weight sank into his own shoulders. ''Those who need the most help don't receive it. Those who want to work hard can't. Instead, they get less.''

An image of Marcelina and Diego entered Isabel's head. "What will the students do?"

Xiloj shrugged impotently. "Suffer."

She knew what that was about.

Xiloj sat wearily on the bank. He looked out and down the hill at the squat school building and at the few children still lingering by the stone walls. "They'll suffer. Like they always do. This is Guatemala."

Isabel looked at the stragglers, too. She cast her feelings outward again, this time trying to let her emotions project from her and dissipate like mist.

"Several years ago," Xiloj said, "before I came here, we went on strike. Do you remember it?"

She recalled only the fact, none of the details.

"Well, you were probably about Marcelina's age. Maybe you don't remember. The strike lasted three months. The districts took turns demonstrating in the capital. The president said he did not want to make any concessions. He didn't want to talk to us. I guess he thought the problem would simply die away if he did nothing. To his credit, he did make an order that there would be no violence and no interference by the army. But he said he would never compromise with the teachers."

"But why?"

"According to him, he was following the wishes of the people. The newspapers said teachers made too much money already and that they weren't very good, anyway. According to some people—really according to him and to certain people in power—everyone was dissatisfied with Guatemala's education. They accused us of not teaching anything to the children."

162

"But you did!"

"Something, anyway."

Isabel felt her frustration rise. "But it's the people who don't always want education for the children. They don't see how good it is. How important."

"You know that better than anyone, I suppose." He did not suppress a proud smile.

Isabel wanted an answer to this, how to make it right, how to change things so that she and others could have what they wanted.

"It's very difficult to argue against the need to have children in the fields. Too many families are just barely able to grow enough to live. A child in school is a child not helping."

"It's not fair!"

"And it's not fair to the students that we go on strike, but we're trying to think of the long range."

"Would it help families pay for school?"

"Partly. Everything needs to get better. The teachers need more training. The students need better food. They need encouragement to come. Both parents and their children need to see how important it is."

"Why can't people see that?"

"Or the president?" he pointed out. "Well, maybe the president does, but it isn't what he said."

"It's unfair."

"Very unfair."

He looked down at the school yard. Isabel could see him thinking.

"That last strike was very bad," he said. "Elections were coming up and the political opposition saw the demonstrations as a chance to embarrass President Porfino. They provoked certain groups against the teachers. Unfortunately, we started blocking the roads into the capital; we wanted to show the country how many of us there were and how everyone needed us. Maybe we wanted to get more people involved, too. Anyway, it ended in disaster. Teachers were attacked. One woman was butchered by young men with machetes. Others were crushed by cars. Later the bombings began. God! A lot of us were arrested. A few died in jail; some disappeared forever.''

''Did they arrest you?''

''I was put in a cell for three weeks.''

Isabel felt a whirling inside her mind and body, something like nausea.

''I was lucky.''

Isabel's lungs gasped for air; her heart battered inside its cage. The world was enveloped in misfortune. Nothing, and no one, was safe. All of them, no matter who, were surrounded by a ring of volcanoes about to erupt or erupting with the promise of violence and destruction.

''They kept me in a dark room and wouldn't let me see or speak to anyone. Later I found out that they had told my family I was dead. Mostly they just threatened me. Said I was going to be shot for being a collaborator with the guerrillas. Other teachers weren't so lucky.''

Isabel fought against the inevitable imagery of his suffering in this new strike. ''Will it happen again?''

Xiloj saw that he was frightening her. ''I'm sorry. No, I don't think it will happen again. Times are different now. It's better now. We have made progress.''

"But what if it does?"

"We have to hope it will get better. We have to try, Isabel."

Andrés Xiloj took her shoulder and sat her down beside him. "When I was a child, I wanted to be a teacher no matter what. It wasn't only that I wanted to have something better than farming, but I really thought I could help Guatemala. I really wanted to help." He harumphed at his romantic notion. "In those days, no one finished school. And in those days, the guerrillas were more real than now."

Isabel looked up in surprise, remembering the young soldier, the steer, and then later when the young man spoke to her in the center.

The teacher looked out at the trees and chuckled. "When I was a boy, I wanted to be like the roadrunner."

Isabel started. She had heard his analogies about birds many times. Usually he said the students should be like quetzales, flying high and free. She had never heard him or anyone else mention the *pájaro haragán* with anything but disdain.

"We think of it as lazy-bird because it doesn't want to fly, but I think there's a better way to look at it. To me, it's the smartest bird. No one can catch it. No one can shoot one. If it flew, people would kill it, so it stays low, hidden, secretive. And it isn't like other birds—turkeys or chickens—who give themselves up to people and peck around the house until they are eaten. Those birds have become slaves."

Isabel chuckled in spite of his solemn tone. It was a little silly to praise the roadrunner.

165

"Yes," he said, "but have you known anyone to catch one of the lazy-birds?"

"No."

"Now you see! It lives the way it wants to. It doesn't fly, but it can. We've all seen it fly up into branches and then down into the bushes, where it disappears. It has chosen to be in the middle. It has chosen neither to fly too high nor to always grovel on the ground in fear."

Isabel smiled warily.

"I admired it as a child."

She still did not believe he was serious. "You wanted to be a roadrunner?"

"Sure."

She glanced quickly around them. "You mean like a guerrilla?"

"No." He weighed his words. "Not causing trouble. Not that. It was something like finding a new way to be what I wanted to be. And understanding the danger of being different. That was it. Knowing that there *is* danger, but not cowering like everyone else because of it. And not trying to be more than I had a right to be, not trying to be superhuman. It was compromising, I suppose. Like the roadrunner: It chooses to be different, but not so different that it gets attacked."

"Like the poc-duck," Isabel said.

"Something like that. Perhaps I'm not explaining well. I'm not sure I really know what I felt then." He smiled at her. "Or now. It's simple to compare animals, but people . . . that's much more complex, much more difficult."

"I know."

"I know you know."

166

Isabel faced out to the trees. The sun shone brightly; the trees and undergrowth directly in front absorbed so much light into their deep green leaves that the whole area was a contrast of brightness and shadow, light and dark: chiaroscuro. With this, the growing midday heat subdued ambient sounds and added a siestalike quiet.

Xiloj broke through her evasion. "Tell me," he said.

With that simple sentence, he unlocked the carefully guarded trove within her, and her words were pulled forth without thought; it was not necessary for her to ask what he meant. "I don't know what to do."

He settled more comfortably.

"I don't know why Lucas is so angry. I don't understand what is happening to me. Or why." Isabel sucked in air to keep her voice from shaking.

"Have you spoken with him?"

She looked up, hoping to find in him permission to dare such a thing. It was what she had wanted all along.

"Speak with him," he said.

"What if he won't?"

"What is it you want?"

"I don't know! I really don't know."

He lifted her hand into his and patted it. "You should ask yourself what you really want, Isabel. It's all right not to know. But ask yourself. Trust yourself. It's also all right to want something. Even to want something different, something no one else wants. There's nothing wrong with that. But try to know what that truly is. It's important to accept yourself and to not be ashamed or afraid of what you are, whatever that is. No one should make you think that what you feel is wrong. No one. And if you want something different from others, you have to accept that. You *can* be different. Trust that! Don't forget it. That's the first and most important step. You don't have to do what everyone else says. It won't be easy for you, but you don't have to kill your hopes. And you may not be able to get what you want, but the worst thing is to live by lying to yourself, by never even trying. That's not living at all! Promise you won't ever do that to yourself. You understand, no? I hope you do. It's very important. Understand it with your bones, Isabel. Understand it with your blood. What matters most is the strength to accept myself.'' Xiloj smirked at his mistake. ''I mean you. Each of us— accepting ourselves. Each of us. You and me.'' His fingers pressed around her hand. ''And then holding on no matter how hard it gets.''

Fifteen

Isabel could not relax enough to keep her right shoulder from spasming just under the skin. Her flesh leaped into frenzied gyrations every few seconds. Her throat felt dry and her stomach gurgled. On uncertain legs she went. On some level she knew that courage is often nothing more than a knot of muscle at the gears of the jaw.

Tracking was second nature to her now. She sniffed along the paths, searched along the roadwork leading out of the village, captured informants who pushed fingers into the air like tremulous arrows, and doggedly followed the narrow paths winding serpentine through cornfields.

She arrived. "I want to talk to you."

Lucas scraped the earth toward him. His hoe skittered across rock. The sun brightened over his back as he bent to lift free a stone. He stepped sideways and reached out with the hoe. *Snick* went the blade. The earth was dry, light brown, white when the sun reflected at a sharp angle. The hoe rasped back toward him and built another small mound alongside the first. A richer brown folded onto the thin topsoil. He stepped sideways and thrust again; the hoe clanked against rock. He shifted to uproot the obstacle. The blade slid sharply into the socket made by the rock. He tugged, but the blade skipped back. Again the thin blade made its incision. The ground relented. Lucas bent and pulled the stone free. He hoed across the pucker and rasped another mound into the row. His foot lifted and fell inches to the left.

"Damn you, Lucas! I want to talk to you!"

Lucas stopped and stared straight ahead, looking way out across the hills and up at Tolimán Volcano, his back to Isabel. He seemed to consider turning: His shoulders slackened for a moment, the shaft of the hoe dropping slowly to his side, but he did not turn.

His face moved inches so that Isabel saw his sharp profile: his eyes held level, his strong nose and rounded lips, the high forehead and firm chin. His was a handsome Mayan face, the kind seen on ancient stelae and murals. The young warrior, the Indian prince, could be seen in the lines of his face. His bare upper body, too, seemed full of Mayan pride: something ancient and proud and astounding; something stretching back through time to the beginnings of a great civilization.

She spoke slowly, without her previous anger, pronouncing everything with absolute certainty. "Lucas, I'm not going to leave until we talk."

A shudder went through him, as if he were struggling with some internal demon. The hoe came up again, high, the blade reaching up past his shoulders and head and into the air like a weapon. When it hit the earth, pebbles and grit exploded out.

Isabel sat down.

The hoe pulled the burst ground back to the row of mounds and went out again. Lucas now raked with such anger that the mounds grew larger, the earth turned browner, his back muscles tightened.

Isabel watched patiently as he tore at the ground more and more ferociously. He stabbed and pulled and stabbed for three meters. The sweat leaped from him. His pants and sash belt soaked up the perspiration that ran from his head and arms and slicked his torso. He didn't bother to wipe his face or stop to rest, but gouged and raked in anger until the perspiration boiled from every pore. And then he turned.

For a second, Isabel thought he would leap on her with the hoe and rake her down into the ground.

"So you love this American!"

"What?"

"Teresa told me—"

"Teresa?" The surprise galvanized her, brought her to her feet.

"I didn't believe it, but I saw you two."

"We were talking, Lucas."

"Why? What do you have to say to him? There's nothing that you should be talking about. Nothing!"

"That's not fair! He's a doctor—"

Lucas stepped forward. "He is not!"

"But he works with them. I mean he knows about them and—"

"And that's why you have to meet with him in se-cret? Didn't your mother tell you not to speak with him? Didn't Teresa tell you that I didn't want you to speak with him? Doesn't that mean anything to you?''

"Lucas, no!" She tried to move forward, to reach for him, but his anger froze her arms and legs. "You know we went to Sololá because of my mother."

He looked past her.

"He's trying to help. Why can't you understand that? Why does it have to be anything else? Why, Lucas?" Despite all her private resolutions not to cry, she broke. Her legs gave in after all her effort. The current in her body snapped, and she shrank to the ground. She brought her shawl up to hide her face. Her gulps for air filled the space between them.

Automatically, Lucas stepped close. His hand snaked out to comfort but stopped in midair. The fingers curled back under like waning petals.

Isabel spoke from the veil of her shawl. "The American means nothing to me."

"Then why did you send him a note to meet you?"

"What?" The shawl came away.

"You sent him a note."

"I did not." Isabel bolted up. "I never sent him any note. Who told you that?"

Lucas crossed his arms. "And you didn't tell Teresa that you wanted to find an American to take you away from here?"

"That's ridiculous. I never said anything like that and I never wrote to him."

"You didn't tell Teresa that you never wanted to marry me?"

"No!"

They stood a few feet apart, glaring at each other.

Isabel saw a tiny sliver of shadow cross his pupils, as if something inside of him were working through a puzzle, pulling apart the pieces that had been handed to him whole and just now, as he stood solidly before her, forging them into another pattern, another consistent form, another possibility.

"Teresa," Isabel whispered, astonished at the thought.

He spun on his heels to look away.

Isabel saw the pieces falling, too. "She still wants you. She wants us apart." She looked at his back. "Did she say it to you?"

Lucas hissed in disbelief.

"My God." Isabel's hands pressed around her head. "She's been telling you things for a long time, hasn't she?" She barely noticed Lucas turning back toward her. It was all unraveling for her. "When I stopped going to school—no, when I couldn't see you as much because my mother got worse, Teresa told you that I didn't want to be married. She told you lies. She turned everything I said into something else. And *she* was the one who left the signs by the house. Why?" She stared harshly at him. "She lied to you. Didn't she?"

He did not need to answer.

"What did she say? What— Why did you believe her?"

His hand rubbed the hair on his nape.

"Why?" Isabel demanded. "How could you?"

He squeezed his brow, his fingers pulling the tension toward the bridge of his nose, easing it out of his face and body.

"Well?"

Desperately, he exploded: "At least she knows that

she loves me! That she wants to be with me! And what she wants!" Just as quickly as the words spurted forth, Lucas knew how stupid it all was, how childish.

But Isabel blushed with understanding. She had never really opened herself completely to him. She always had this thing inside her making a wall. Even when she felt attracted to him, so that her skin and belly tingled with longing, there was this ring of mountains that kept all but a few safe words from drifting between them. That was the real reason he had believed Teresa. He needed to feel something clear and unambiguous—unwavering love. Isabel tried to meet his pleading eyes. She saw in them a quiet prayer for a rain of words that would erode the wall between them, words that had to rain down from *her,* words that she had never given to him easily. He would let it all go if she would simply commit.

Even with this knowledge, her shawl, defiantly, crept up and over her mouth. Her eyes dropped.

Lucas staggered back as if he had been struck by a fist to his chest.

Just then, Isabel's name rang out from below. It came again, and a third time before they both turned to see José running toward them. His voice climbed up to where they stood, broke through the hard silence between them, and reached their ears in shreds: ". . . very bad again! Hurry! Can't you hear me?" José stopped and yanked through the air with his arm to tell her to come. "Hurry up!"

Isabel faced Lucas. Her mouth moved, twitched as if to speak. His whole body seemed to lean into her with expectation, his eyes longing for a sign that only she could give, that she *must* give to regain anything between them.

174

José called again, angrily, raking through their silence.

"I have to go," she whispered.

Isabel and José ran hard to their home. They drew the attention of people in the street, of neighbors and friends. Panting, they arrived to find Diego and Marcelina pressed against a wall. Their father held their mother's head in the crook of his arm, his head bent sorrowfully low; their mother's legs splayed out before her. José stopped dead still. Isabel cried out and dropped trembling beside her father. Mercifully, before Alfredo spoke, Manuela opened her eyes.

None of them noticed, at first, the people gathering at the door, bulging slowly inward. "Is she all right?" Josefa asked.

Alfredo looked up, his face uncertain.

A young man, nearly hidden in the back, said, "Eziquel is at the home of Salvador Cawek."

"Go," someone commanded.

Alfredo lifted his hand to stop him, and drew it back to cover his mouth. The neighbor women tightened their circle. They peered down. More people entered to see what all the commotion was about.

"She needs air," Isabel said. "Room."

The women ignored her and pressed closer. Some of the women, those who had come days before with Josefa, shouldered their way forward. All of them seemed intent on seeing what the situation was so that they could offer their medical advice. It burst from them:

"Put cold water on her forehead."

"Raise her feet above her head."

The wall of prescribers loomed nearer.

"Father, she needs room."

Alfredo settled his wife higher into his arms, his face nestling protectively against her hair.

"Give her water."

"Let her smell garlic."

Diego and Marcelina were no longer visible because of the gathered crowd. José stood mutely nearby, so that Isabel and her father crouched together with Manuela between them.

Again Isabel felt the observers shrinking the space around them. "She needs room."

Her mother came suddenly alert; she jerked forward and clutched her hands to her chest. "Ow!" she moaned.

"Give her something to drink!"

She doubled forward, her right hand prodding her chest as if she were trying to work something loose just under her skin. Her face twisted with each sharp pang.

"Give her room!" Isabel pleaded.

The watchers inched forward.

By the door, Eziquel shouted "Out!" His voice broke through like the screech of an eagle, and it forced open a space for him to enter. "Go outside!" he commanded. "Out, everyone!"

The crowd drew back. They pulled apart and moved heavily outside, Eziquel prodding them with his commandments to leave.

Manuela's face suddenly paled. Isabel saw her neck quiver, and she recognized that her mother could not breathe. Her mouth contorted; a bubble appeared between her lips. Her fingers at her chest were like hen claws, frantically clutching. The coloring in her hands drained away, and her eyes convulsed under the lids.

Without thinking or hearing, Isabel had one of the capsules in her fingers. She crushed it and pushed the vial under her mother's nose. "Breathe!" she shouted, so loudly that it stopped everyone—those already outside; those moving reluctantly out to give Manuela room; Eziquel, moving forward and down; Alfredo, who seemed to be falling backward and away from the terrible center of his dying wife.

The small perfume of amyl nitrite leaked through the channels of Manuela's body to her chambered heart, where it erupted. Manuela gasped and rolled away from her daughter's hand. Then Isabel and Alfredo smelled the sharp medicine.

Eziquel continued forward until he knelt beside Isabel's mother. He took her hand, checked her pulse and eyes. "Get out!" he screamed at the remaining onlookers. His face was a snarl over his shoulder, but when he turned back to Alfredo, something docile came over him. "Let me help," he said. The two men lifted Manuela up from the floor.

Isabel stayed seated on the ground. She sat still, the crushed, netted capsule in her palm. She remained quiet and seated as everyone moved out of the house and down the avenue. She sat immobile until her mother was comfortable in bed between her father and Eziquel. And then she looked up. Lucas stood patiently by the door, waiting for her to see him. His face revealed nothing. He stared for a moment; then he turned away. The sun poured into the place he had occupied. Beside that bright space where Lucas had waited, Marcelina and

Diego clutched at each other. Their small, frightened faces almost made her cry. She sucked in air to fight it off.

Alfredo asked her to get water. When she did not move, he called again. She arose from the ground and mechanically poured a glass. Manuela bravely smiled at her from the bed, this attack now safely over. Yet her father absently rubbed his throat, and his eyes combatted fears he did not want to show. Don Eziquel stroked Manuela's arm.

"She should take the medicine," Isabel said flatly, resolutely.

Her mother's smile disappeared. She shook her head. "Yes, Mother."

Behind Manuela, Alfredo nodded so minutely that Isabel nearly missed his private oath to her.

"No," Manuela feebly said, her face turning away to the wall.

Both Alfredo and Eziquel nodded, assuring Isabel that Manuela would take the medicine.

Isabel stood by Marcelina and Diego. She lovingly caressed the fear of death out through Marcelina's hair. Her little sister fell into Isabel's skirt. Diego remained rigid beside them, his back pressed against the wall, his expression blank as he looked up at his stony brother, José. Isabel could see the lava of emotion flowing in his young eyes, the ground shifting inside him, and yet she knew that this very movement of emotion would heave up a ring of implacable hills meant to protect and hide the deep lake of feelings nestled within him. José stood rock still and apart, already comfortable with silence and manhood and a tightly fortified self.

Isabel glanced once more at her mother, resting safely between her father and Eziquel. Her father's expression revealed nothing. Eziquel sat quiet and still. Inside herself, she felt the mask of silent endurance coming up.

Before it fit snugly over her real face, Isabel turned and left the room. The gate closed behind her, and anxious wings sprouted. She ran furiously down to the path leading up to the center, hoping like mad that she would find Lucas before he walked so far away that he would never come back, no matter what words came out of her.

She saw him where the two paths met. He had been waiting for her, squatting on his heels in the shade, looking up toward her house. A large *hormigo* tree loomed behind him. She moved up to him without speaking, clumsily turning the used capsule in her hand, fidgeting as she tried to straighten her thoughts. Her mind was a jumble that prevented speech, a whirlpool of words and gestures that just would not arrange themselves. She stood mute before him. His face studied hers; it squinted with expectation, but nothing came from her mouth, and he turned away. His whole body instantly tensed, forcing Isabel to follow his gaze.

Teresa walked toward them like a sleepwalker. Her feet lifted and fell awkwardly; her arms hung too limply at her sides, so that Isabel glanced above her, half expecting to see puppet strings dangling from the sky. Teresa looked at Isabel, not at Lucas. She stepped nearer, her face twisted into disbelief and torment and pleading.

So much fear emanated from Teresa that the desire to strike her came and went rapidly in Isabel. Instead, she faced Lucas.

"I love you," she said loudly, clearly, each word coming from her throat with a deep thudding of her heart.

He glanced up.

How strong the words' aftertaste in her body—as if they were some pouring forward, some flooding that could inundate them both. The second time the words came easier. "I love you," she proclaimed.

Lucas flew up, his hands reaching up and out, touching her hands, gliding smoothly up her arms, electrifying her shoulders, cupping her ears in the warmth of his embrace. When he pressed his lips to hers, it was as if nothing ever had been wrong between them. The capstone at her throat lifted away and the well deep inside her heart brimmed up and filled her mouth with soft sounds that mimicked the uninhibited bubbling of the lake.

Teresa stood in the sun like a trap marker.

Isabel swayed with the force of his kiss, giving in to his urgency. He had lifted out her small capstone and thrust it heavenward, where it grew into a protective shelter above them. Yet when his body pleaded for hers, she slipped her hand to the top of his chest and pushed his lips away. The obsidian of his eyes shone inches from hers.

"I want to be a teacher," she whispered.

His whole body stiffened.

"Lucas?"

His hands dropped from her waist.

"Lucas," she whispered, "I want to be your wife."

He looked like a child listening to punishment in the guise of love.

"I mean it."

"Isabel—" he began.

"I love you!" She felt the heat of her face again. The blush of something real and necessary. Something dangerous. "I want to be your wife. I want us to be married. But I want you to help me become a teacher."

The line of his mouth drew straight.

"I want this," she said.

Lucas's eyes blinked shut.

"With you. I want to be a teacher and I want to be with you."

It was impossible. It was asking too much. It was crazy. "How, Isabel?" His voice groaned with weariness.

She yanked him closer. "I want to try." She kissed his lips. "I want you to help me. As my husband, Lucas."

He looked past her eyes and up into the hills. "I don't know how we can do it."

"I just want to try."

"It'll cost too much. Where will we get the money?"

"I don't know."

"You'll have to go to another city to study. We'll be apart."

She curled his attention back to her with the tips of her fingers. "We can do that."

"What kind of marriage is that? We won't be like a normal husband and wife."

"I know."

"What about your mother?"

"I'll care for her."

"And your family?"

"Also."

He moved helplessly under her determination. "How can we do it?"

"I don't know, Lucas."

"I don't know either."

Isabel glided a finger across his lips. "All I want is for you to tell me we'll try. No matter what."

"I don't know how—"

"Just tell me we'll try. That we will really try. That's all I want, Lucas. Just that first step."

He looked out at the mountains surrounding the lake. A few afternoon clouds were just appearing among the peaks, leaking slowly down into the rifts between the cones like white water through stony channels. But her fierce determination pulled him back into her.

Lucas spoke quietly in the space between their mouths. "I love you."

Her fingers tightened around his, pleading still for this step, for this first understanding no matter how inscrutable the future.

"I don't know how we can do it."

She held still, wanting him to come toward her now, the way she had come toward him.

"I don't know," he said.

Her words fluttered out from her. "Just tell me we'll try."

"I don't think it will be—"

"It won't be easy!"

"How will—"

"We'll try!"

He felt his eyes batting. His neck throbbed with some new emotion, something without a name yet. The air before his eyes seemed to pop and sparkle, like it had when he flipped head over heels to make his goal. In that instant, he had seen the world upside down. In a brief gasp of time, he had seen the world as he had never conceived of it. It was a vision of how things might be different—not necessarily the only other way things had to be, but simply that the world didn't have to be what he always saw with his feet planted on the ground, his shoulders arced to some labor, his eyes and lungs choked with dust. There, in Isabel's face, he could see a dream of a completely different angling of the world.

"Okay," he said. "I promise."

Isabel's face brightened, and she reached out to him. Their bodies enfolded one into the other, arms looping, limbs meshing, till they were like a single body on the path. Enveloped in each other's arms, they did not care about the bitter girl rooted so close. Nor did they concern themselves with the two boys running and calling out the news that a commissioner had been killed in Santiago Atitlán. The boys' movement past them was like the blur of hummingbirds, their shouts the cawing of crows. And the girl with stars in her mouth blurred away, too, so that within their passionate embrace, all they cared about was that, nestled among the volcanoes of Guatemala, there existed a hope with a secret pair of wings.

About the Author

Omar S. Castañeda was born in Guatemala and grew up in the U.S. He has returned to Guatemala many times in order to study life in Mayan villages. About this book he says: "Because I am Guatemalan-American and have always lived in non-Hispanic communities in the U.S., I have had to deal with conflicting views of the world. In my writing, I investigate the individual's search for identity in a changing world. My characters glimpse something other than what is sanctioned by their native culture, and at the same time, they value many of their society's traditions."

Mr. Castañeda is the author of a novel for adults, *Cunuman,* and the editor of an anthology, *New Visions: Fiction by Florida Writers.* He lives in Bellingham, Washington, where he teaches at Western Washington University. He is married and has two children.